THE SONG
OF THE DEAD

"Where are you going?" rapped Dr James as Kit Mason turned towards the blazing building.

"Inside!" he yelled over his shoulder.

"Why?" asked Barney. "What the hell for?"

"There's a glass container with some rats in it. I'm going to get them out. I think that's the only cage Tommy left intact."

Barney stared at him in amazement as he dashed back.

Alice stood up shakily, holding her head. "Where's he gone?"

"Back inside."

"No! What for?"

"To rescue some rats."

"Rats! So he was right after all," she said in distress. "He *was* fooling Dr James. He *was* taking photographs. We shouldn't have doubted him."

Look out for:

The Ferryman's Son by Ian Strachan

THE SONG OF THE DEAD

by
ANTHONY MASTERS
Illustrated by Max Schindler

Hippo Books
Scholastic Publications Limited
London

Scholastic Publications Ltd,
10 Earlham Street, London WC2H 9RX, UK

Scholastic Inc,
730 Broadway, New York, NY 10003, USA

Scholastic Tab Publications Ltd,
123 Newkirk Road, Richmond Hill,
Ontario L4C 3G5, Canada

Ashton Scholastic Pty Ltd,
P O Box 579, Gosford, New South Wales,
Australia

Ashton Scholastic Ltd,
165 Marua Road, Panmure, Auckland 6,
New Zealand

First published by Scholastic Publications Ltd., 1990

ISBN 0 590 76280 X

Typeset by AKM Associates (UK) Ltd, Southall, London
Printed by Cox & Wyman Ltd, Reading, Berks

Chapter One

Barney was intrigued by the cottage from the very first. Made of clapboard, it leant rather crazily against a warehouse right at the end of their back garden. Originally painted white, it was now a battered grey. The roof was covered in pitch and a stovepipe chimney clung to the topmost part, looking as if it might come off at any moment.

"Shall I go and see what they're like?" he had asked his father on the day they moved in.

"No, Barney. Leave them alone. Folks keep themselves to themselves in little towns like this. Give them a chance to come to us." But they never had and Barney had only had glimpses of the girl next door. She was very striking, with long blonde hair and a strong, square face. She made fleeting appearances, but every time Barney walked down the scrubby little garden she vanished into her tumbledown house.

Barney Hampton's parents were renting the cottage in Whitstable for six months while they illustrated a book about sailing barges. They were both artists and the commission was important enough for them to need to be on the spot. They had arrived in the Easter holidays and tomorrow Barney was starting at the local comprehensive for a term before they all returned to London. He wasn't looking forward to starting a new school in such a temporary sort of way, and already he was missing his friends. His parents had tried to persuade him to go to the local youth club but he had hung back, putting off meeting anyone new. It was difficult being an only child. You had to do everything by yourself.

Mooching around at home, he became fascinated by the girl at the bottom of the garden. She never seemed to go out. He reckoned that she was about fifteen – a year or so older than himself – and the more she kept her distance the more he wanted to contact her. He knew that the family had a fishing boat in the harbour and that it was owned by her father and older brother. There was no sign of a mother.

Today, Barney decided, he was definitely going to speak to her. Her father and brother always went down to the harbour at dawn and never returned until evening. Was she shut up there all on her own? he wondered. He was determined to think of a good excuse to visit her, and at about eleven o'clock he hit upon a brilliant one. Both his parents were out drawing, and his bicycle tyre was flat and the pump didn't work. An ideal excuse. Rather nervously Barney began to walk down the narrow alley that led to the fisherman's clapboard house. As he made his short journey, he could see the estuary quiet and flat in front of him. Whitstable was a small working town by the sea with a harbour and a modest fishing fleet. Barney felt a surge of elation. The town felt good. Perhaps he would be able to fit in here after all, especially if he could get to know this elusive girl.

When he arrived, he couldn't find much sign of a front door. The garden was a jumble of rotting nets, broken-down bicycles and a couple of old prams, and there was a strong smell of fish and a large number of rusting buckets and tackle. Walking round the paint-peeling walls he eventually found a side door and knocked. It was a lovely spring morning and the beginnings of a fresh breeze stirred against his cheeks. He knocked again. Still there was no reply. Then he noticed that the door was slightly ajar. He pushed and it opened to reveal a tiny hallway that led into the darkness of a room behind. Barney called out:

"Is anyone home?" Still no answer, but he thought he detected a slight movement.

There was a faint rustle and then a kind of waiting silence.

"Is anyone home?"

Still the waiting silence.

"Is anyone home?" he asked for the third time, beginning to feel really scared. The hallway smelt stuffy and there was a shut-in feeling to the house as if nobody ever opened any windows. The noise came again from the living room, and with sudden determination he moved forward. The shut-in smell became even more intense. He paused, called again and then slowly walked towards the open door. Barney froze on the threshold for what seemed like ages. Then he crept inside.

The room was literally stuffed with furniture and there were old newspapers and magazines all over the floor and a big, scarred table. An old gramophone lay in bits near a sagging sofa and some dirty clothes were flung in a basket. Heavy curtains were drawn against the gloriously fresh morning, but to Barney's intense shock he was just able to pick out a figure crouched behind an armchair. It was the girl.

"I won't hurt you," he whispered, instinctively feeling a loud voice would terrify her even more. She was dirty and scruffy and there was a bruise on the side of her cheek. She stared back at him over the arm of the chair, looking like a frightened animal.

"What are you doing in our house?" Her voice was low and rough, as if she didn't speak very much, but she sounded defiant, even accusing.

"The door was open," he said lamely.

"Do you usually come into people's houses without an invitation?" The accusing note had deepened.

"I tried knocking at the door, but you didn't answer."

4

"I didn't *want* to answer. You should have gone away."

"Are you all right?" Barney blurted out, beginning to feel silly. Worse still, he knew now that he was just an unwelcome intruder. So much for his plans to get to know this strange girl! And on top of all that, his reason for coming now seemed incredibly feeble.

"Of course I'm all right." She scowled at him, her eyes hard and bright, and he drew back a little.

"I just wanted to borrow a bike pump. I thought you might have one."

"A what?"

"A pump."

"Why should we have a pump?" She made it sound as if he wanted to borrow half a tonne of cement.

"Well –" Barney's voice tailed away while he thought about that one. "You've got plenty of bikes round here," he added hopefully.

"They're all broken. So we don't need no pumps, do we?"

Barney had to admit the wisdom of that, but he was determined to persevere. "Anyway, I wanted to meet you."

"Why?"

"We just moved in."

"No you didn't. You moved in last week."

"So what? I just wanted to get to know people. Like you."

"Well, I don't want to get to know you, do I?"

The conversation, thought Barney, was going

nowhere fast. "Thanks a lot," he said, trying not to feel hurt.

"Now get out."

"You all right?" She was still crouched by the chair.

"I said get out!"

"I just wanted to . . ."

"Get out or I'll belt you!"

"You? Belt me?" He laughed uneasily as she stayed where she was.

"Get out!" she hissed.

"You're not very polite, are you?"

"Get out!" She spat the words at him and finally Barney decided to give up.

"All right. I'm going."

"And don't come back. We don't like your type."

" 'Type'? What do you mean, 'type'?" he said, suddenly feeling angry.

"People who break into other people's houses. You wait till I tell my Dad. And Jamie."

"Who's Jamie?" But he knew. He just wanted to keep her talking. Somehow. Anyhow.

"My brother."

"Tell them what you like," said Barney, trying unsuccessfully to sound casual. "But I didn't break in. The door was open and –"

"Get out! Go on! Get out!" But still she made no attempt to move away from behind the armchair.

Barney looked at her with angry bewilderment. Their eyes locked. Then he turned away abruptly and walked quickly out of the room. As he went he yelled:

"I don't want to stay anyway." He knew he sounded childish, but it was the only thing that he could think of saying.

Barney stumbled back up the alley, close to tears. Why did she despise him so much? It wasn't fair. He hadn't done anything wrong in going into their dump of a house and he wasn't going to apologise to anyone. He certainly wasn't going to tell his parents about what had happened. They would only make a fuss, particularly Dad. Barney knew that Dad would have hated anyone barging in like that. But he didn't need human company. He was always lost in his work and as for playing with Barney – well, it had never happened. He hardly even spoke to him.

Mum was different. She was a big woman with a mop of unruly long black hair, and Barney had once had a fight with a boy at his last school because he had called her a gypsy. Mum didn't care what she looked like. Neither did Dad, come to that, but Mum was much more fun. She liked to try out things that she had never done. Together they had gone ice-skating and trampolining and tobogganing. She always fell down or off, but Mum reckoned that was all part of the fun and she never minded when she got laughed at. She didn't even seem to notice. But now she was so wrapped up in the book that down there in Whitstable she had done nothing with him at all. This made him very lonely and was another reason why Barney was determined not to tell either of his parents what had happened. They just didn't deserve to know, he thought, miserably. He had never felt so isolated in his life, and there was the new school to face tomorrow as well.

As he reached his own front door, his mother's words rang in his ears: "This is very important, this book. It's important to us all. If it comes off we'll have a reputation at last and – just as important – a decent amount of money for a change. So you'll have to be patient with us." But Barney was fed up with being patient – fed up to the back teeth. And now this had to go and happen, just to make him feel even more alone than before.

His mother's voice faded, to be replaced by the girl who had been so strangely angry. "Get out!" she said. "Just get out!" And her voice kept on shouting at him in his mind.

Barney spent the rest of the day mooning about and staring out of the window at the tumbledown cottage at the end of the garden. After a while he began to wonder if she would come out. But she didn't, and towards teatime he fell asleep in front of the television.

He dreamt that instead of rejecting him so violently she had answered his knock and invited him in to tea. What a tea it was! Doughnuts and six different kinds of sandwiches and buns with chocolate spread or strawberry jam and pork pies and fruit cake and Coke and . . . Barney woke from his dream abruptly to see a man on the television screen making an omelette. Realising he was hungry, he went to the kitchen and made himself a boring ham sandwich. The bread was stale and the ham thin and tasteless. There wasn't even any mustard, because Mum had run out as usual. She wasn't a very methodical housekeeper – in fact, she wasn't much of a house-keeper at all.

Eventually Barney's parents returned, tired and snappy with each other. It was soon clear to him that they had some kind of disagreement during the day's work, and both slumped sulkily in front of the television. Soon his father was asleep and snoring and his mother was pouring herself a second glass of gin.

"Goodnight, Mum," said Barney, getting up abruptly.

"Goodnight, love." She gave him an absentminded and gin-scented kiss. "Had a good day?" she asked as an afterthought.

"Great," he replied bleakly.

"What did you do?" Suddenly she was staring at him questioningly and he realised with a spurt of pleasure that she did care after all.

"Mucked about."

"What does that mean?"

"Nothing."

"We thought you'd be bored if we took you with us."

9

"Sure. I was happier here."

"Mucking about?" She sipped at her gin. "Anyway," she suddenly seemed to brighten, "you'll make some friends tomorrow, won't you? When you go to school."

"You bet!" said Barney with forced cheerfulness, and went up to bed.

It was worse than he had imagined. The school was a big concrete shell on a windswept estate near the sea. The teachers seemed nice though, and so far they had all been very welcoming. Not so the kids. Barney had lunch on his own while they chattered around him and none of them made the slightest attempt to speak to him. They weren't like London kids, he thought. They were clannish and there seemed a hostility to them – a suspicion of anyone new or anything different. After lunch, Barney mooched around in the playground until he was suddenly conscious of a small crowd of boys. They were about his own age and they were staring at him. At first he brightened up because he thought they might be coming over to make friends, but when he saw their faces he decided they very definately weren't. Then one of the boys detached himself from the crowd. He was bigger than Barney and had a hard look to him. His face was weatherbeaten and his hair was cut very short.

"You Hampton?"

"Yes."

"You been thieving, then?"

"Eh?" Barney stared at him, uncomprehendingly.

"You went in my cousin's place." His voice had hardened.

"I don't know what you're talking about," said Barney defensively. But of course he knew exactly what he was talking about. He stared round him. Unfortunately they had caught at him at the side of the playground that faced over the marshes, well away from the school buildings. They must have been biding their time. Barney knew that he stood no chance against them. Desperately, hopelessly, he tried to walk back towards the school, but they only moved in, surrounding him in a semi-circle.

The big boy came closer. "You shouldn't have done that."

"I still don't know what you're talking about." Barney was determined to play innocent for as long as he could, but time was running out.

"She was upset, see?"

"Who?"

"My cousin. When you bust in on her."

"I didn't."

The boy came nearer and Barney could smell his breath. "You scared her out of her wits."

"Oh, that –" He tried to sound casual and failed. "The door was open."

"So you *did* go in?"

Barney could see the look of pleasure in the eyes of the other kids; the hunt was scenting blood.

"I wanted to borrow a pump – a bike pump." A howl of derisive laughter went up but Barney struggled on. "So I knocked and there was no reply and then I walked down the hall into the living room and she was there." He ended in a rush.

"What was she doing?" The boy's voice was sharp.

"I – I think she was hiding behind a chair," he replied feebly.

"I wouldn't find that surprising, would you?" He was even closer now and began to poke at Barney's chest with a stubby finger. "I expect she thought you was one of them muggers. Eh?"

"I told you. I just wanted to borrow a pump."

Another howl of laughter went up, but this time there was more anger than derision in it.

"You know my name?"

"Why should I?" stammered Barney.

"It's Darren. That's my name. It's a name you won't forget in a hurry."

"I don't get you. I didn't touch her. I went to borrow a –"

"What's my name?" The forefinger jabbed even more fiercely.

"Darren," repeated Barney in a thread of a voice.

"Darren who?"

"What?"

"Darren sir to you."

Barney said nothing.

"Come on."

Still Barney said nothing and Darren suddenly slapped him round the face. The blow stung and Barney felt sick.

"Come on!"

But Barney was determined not to say anything at all now.

"Come on! What are you going to call me?"

Still he said nothing.

Darren slapped him again and as Barney reeled back from the much harder blow he saw the light of pleasure in the eyes around him. There was an electric excitement in the air and a rising sense of anticipation.

"Go away," said Barney miserably. "Leave me alone."

"What's that?"

"I said leave me alone." Barney was whispering now.

"You speaking to me?" Darren pushed his pimply face a centimetre away from his own.

"Yes."

"Thief."

"I'm no thief."

"Course you are. Mugging my cousin."

"I didn't touch her!" Suddenly anger overcame Barney's fear and apprehension.

"Call me sir." His face was almost touching Barney's now.

"Go to hell!"

Darren came at him swinging and Barney lowered his head to ward off the punches and slaps. Then in desperation he grabbed at Darren's legs and they both went down on the hard tarmac. They rolled over only once before Darren was on top, straddling him, his knees pressing down on Barney's shoulders. His weight was unbearable as he started to slap him round the face again.

"Stop that!"

Darren did not look up but continued to rain blows on Barney's face.

The welcome voice came again but nearer now. "Stop that immediately!" When he looked up Barney could see a tall, youngish man with a shock of prematurely grey hair and a hooked nose. Slowly, carelessly, Darren levered himself off Barney and the crushing weight was withdrawn. He struggled to his feet as the young man said: "Now, what's all this about?"

"He attacked my cousin, sir," said Darren respectfully, while the others drew back.

"He *what*?" The young man looked incredulous.

"I didn't attack anyone!" yelled Barney, and began to go through a stumbling explanation.

"I'll see you both in my room. Now," the man said.

Darren went in first and came out grinning after what seemed like hours. Then Barney was summoned.

"Barney Hampton, isn't it?"

"Yes, sir."

"My name's Chris Wharton." The young teacher looked at him kindly and Barney felt a great rush of reassurance. "I'm your head of year. I'm sorry that I haven't got round to seeing you yet. How did all this happen? And what's Darren talking about? That you broke into his cousin's house?"

Barney told him his version of the story more confidently now and the teacher listened carefully.

"Do you believe me, sir?" Barney concluded miserably.

He nodded. "I believe you. I knew Alice Miller when she was here in the First Year. She made a brief appearance."

"She doesn't go to school?" Barney was calmer now but his face was hurting and he felt totally confused.

"Not now. It's against the law, of course, but the law doesn't work."

"What does she do all day?"

"Sits in the cottage. Roves around the beach. But she never leaves the house for long."

"Why?"

Chris Wharton looked at Barney as if he were wondering whether to go on. "It's as though she's always waiting for something to happen." He hesitated. "As though if she leaves the house for a minute it'll disappear."

"How weird."

"Yes. It's been on my mind ever since she left. I arranged for a social worker to go round there but she got short shrift from the old man. There are too many truants round here for one more to matter that much. Anyway," he paused, "the reason I'm telling you all this is that you should steer clear of that family. The old man is brutish and rude, his son is completely under his thumb and Alice is – well, Alice."

"And Darren?"

"He's a vicious little thug. Steer clear of him too, and if he gives you any trouble come and see me. Right away."

"Yes. OK," replied Barney hesitantly, making a mental note to avoid him.

"I realise they live near you and that you were only looking for a friend. And I know how difficult it must be for you, moving down here for such a short time. But even so, be warned. They're a funny bunch and they keep themselves to themselves." He paused. "You'll make friends here. Are you going to join the football club?"

But all the time he was talking Barney was thinking about Alice. Well, at least she had a name now and his fight with Darren was receding into a hastily despatched past. He nodded, trying to help the teacher along, but inwardly Barney's determination grew. He didn't want to join the football club. He just wanted to make friends with Alice.

"Wait a minute." Mr Wharton's voice broke into his thoughts.

"Yes?"

"Your face. I didn't realise –" He sounded very agitated now. "He's really marked you. That's one hell of a bruise!"

"It doesn't matter."

"I'm not putting up with this. He really can't go around –"

Barney interrupted him quickly. "It'll make things worse for me, sir, if you make a fuss."

"But your parents –"

16

"I'll explain it to them." All that Barney wanted to do now was to go. To go and think about Alice.

"We have certain responsibilities to –"

"Please, sir, I'll explain it to them."

Chapter Two

That evening Barney had a quick tea, gave his mother an edited résumé of his day at school, hoping that his bruises didn't show, and went up to his room. He stood by the window, watching Alice's cottage as he now called it. He thought of her again and again, crouched by the chair, telling him to get out. If only she had been asking him to come in instead! He would help her and solve her problems and take her away from her wicked father. Every time he thought of Mr Miller he saw him as some kind of Victorian villain. His son was a shadowy, lesser sort of villain. And he rescued her from both. He didn't think about Darren; he wasn't the kind of person you brought into a waking fantasy. He was too brutal, too real.

Barney must have stayed by the window for over

half an hour, but nothing happened and no one came out or went into the house. He supposed that she was inside but there was no sign of her at all. It was strange that he so desperately wanted to see her after she had treated him so badly and after what Darren had done to him, but he did and he knew that he must stop dreaming and risk everything to see her if he could. But the view from the window became more and more still until he could have been looking at a photograph.

Suddenly he could no longer bear just standing there, alone in his room. He must do something. Go somewhere. Exhaust himself. Barney went downstairs.

"Just going out, Mum."

"Wait a minute!" It was his father's voice.

"I was going out for a bit." Barney was immediately defensive.

"We shan't keep you for long," was the firm response.

Barney wandered reluctantly into the big whitewashed kitchen. What a contrast this was to the dinginess and squalor of the Miller living room. He shook his head irritably. If he thought about that girl again he'd go barmy! But he did think about her – all the time. He just couldn't get her out of his mind.

They were sitting at the table in what he called their "parenting position". Suddenly Barney felt worried. Could they have found out what had happened? That would be the last straw. He would run away and never come back. Or at least he would stay out late and give them a good scare. But there was a look of concern in his parents' eyes and he realised that he was wrong and they knew nothing.

"Barney," his father cleared his throat, "I think we've been neglecting you."

Have you only just found that out? Barney thought with a sudden burst of anger.

His father continued in an apologetic tone while his mother watched him with studied concentration. Had she put him up to it? Barney wondered. Was it really coming from Dad first-hand? Somehow he doubted it – he was far too self absorbed.

"We've dragged you down here and you don't know anyone and we expected you to go to a new school and all that and we don't think it's fair." He finished in a rush. "Do we?" he added, turning to Barney's mother.

She nodded agreement. "That bruise," she said slowly. "Where did you get it?"

"Just messing about in the playground."

"Fighting?"

"Playing a wall game."

She looked at him suspiciously but said no more.

His father continued: "So we've come to a decision."

"Yeah?" It was Barney's turn to be suspicious.

"If you stay at your Auntie May's you could go back to London. You could go back to your old school, and we'll be home as soon as we can. We've discussed the book and we reckon that we can finish it far quicker than we previously thought."

"No thanks."

"What?" They both looked amazed and Barney almost laughed. He'd really caught them out this time.

"No." Barney sounded almost defiant. "I'd rather stay here. Thanks all the same."

"But you've been saying –" His father looked bewildered.

"I made some friends at school today, and I'd rather stay." He said it very quickly, hoping he would be believed.

His parents seemed at a loss for words.

"I'm just going down the road to play football with one of my new mates." Barney spoke with increasing confidence. He looked from one to the other, seeing they were immediately happier, taking it all in. "I'll be getting along, then."

"Wait." His father stood up. "There's something else. I was talking to the woman who runs the little store on the corner and she said something we thought you should know."

"What's that?"

"Those peculiar people at the bottom of the garden. The fisherman – Miller –"

"What about them?"

"You said you wanted to get to know them. Well, our advice is don't." He ended abruptly.

"Why not?"

"Miller drinks." His father sounded rather smug. "He's a lonely, violent sort of man. He beats both his children and one of them – the girl you wanted to

21

meet – well, she's a real problem. Won't go to school. Won't –"

"I don't want to see them anyway," said Barney casually. "I've got friends now."

"Good," said his mother. "We want you to make friends here. We're glad you have?"

"Steer clear of the Millers," said his father, sounding like Mr Wharton.

"Don't worry, Dad," replied Barney. "I will."

Barney walked along the sea wall towards the marshes. It was a lovely spring evening with the sun beginning to set, glowing on the still water of the estuary. The wall ended and he continued along a pebble ridge. As he walked Barney grew angrier and angrier. If the Millers were left to themselves and never given any help, Alice would remain the prisoner she was. It just wasn't fair.

Now he was on marshy grass and the estuary gradually seemed to narrow. Below him was a muddy beach on which a number of old hulks were drawn up. It was low tide and the sandy mud stretched several kilometres out to the waterline. Some of the hulks were complete wrecks; others were in better condition and one or two looked as if they might be lived in. But there was only one that had smoke curling out of a stack on its roof.

Barney paused. The old barge looked very cosy in the twilight, with its varnished sides and newly painted railings. Then he heard the whining. At first it was low-pitched and hard to hear, but the more he listened the more Barney realised that something must be wrong. He looked around him, but there was no one in sight. The last thing he wanted was to trespass again, but the whining was growing louder. What should he do? Then Barney decided: he would knock and hope someone would come. If they didn't he would go and get help. But he was definitely not going to open the door. He had opened Alice Miller's door, and look what had happened to him after that!

Desperately Barney took another glance around him but there was still no sign of anyone at all. The whining had now become a howl and it was unbearable to listen to. He *had* to do something. He ran over the plank between shore and barge and began to bang at the door. There was no reply and he was forcibly reminded of the Millers' cottage. He stood there indecisively, but the howling had now reached such a pitch that all his resolutions about not opening the door deserted him. He just couldn't bear it any longer. Without thinking about the consequences any more, Barney pushed at the door of the barge.

The door wouldn't budge. Barney pushed at it again and again before he realised it was locked. He paused, knowing that he would have to get in somehow. He edged forward and cautiously worked his way around the narrow deck. There was barely enough room for him to kneel down and try to look through the porthole, but eventually he succeeded. Barney immediately let out a gasp of dismay.

The cabin was full of water and a large Alsatian dog

lay on the floor, partly submerged. Barney tapped at the window and the dog's eyes turned to him, helpless and appealing. Why didn't the dog move? he wondered. There must be a hole in the floor through which the water was coming. He got up from his crouching position. The tide was coming in and more water must be slowly trickling into the barge. Soon it would be too late to do anything and the dog would drown.

Again Barney stared helplessly at the shore but there was not a soul about. The barge gave a sudden lurch beneath his feet and when Barney looked through the porthole window again, he saw the water was surging up. Soon it could be over the Alsatian's head.

Barney hurried round to the stern. There was a hatch and he wondered if he could break it open. At first he tried pulling at it, but he knew that he wasn't strong enough. Then he kicked at it viciously, and with satisfaction heard it beginning to give in a splintering of wood. Still without any thought of the consequences he continued to kick at the flimsy structure. As he did so the Alsatian started to howl again. It was unbearable and Barney redoubled his efforts. Finally the hatch gave way and Barney almost fell into the musty interior. There was a strange smell in there and he knew it couldn't just be sea water. Could it be the Alsatian's fear?

Barney whistled, but although the dog looked at him with imploring eyes it made no move. Realising it was trapped, Barney hurried to its side and began to grope about underneath the water. He found the dog's paw and as he held it the dog gave a pathetic moan, horribly human in its desperation. He tugged at the paw but it seemed wedged in the water-logged planking. As he wrenched at it something floated up. It was a seaman's cap and it bobbed up and down beside him as he tried to prise the paw out of its trap.

Water was bubbling even more furiously into the long, narrow cabin and it was already up to his knees. He wrenched again at the paw but it was still stuck fast. Who could have abandoned the animal to such a plight? Anger made Barney pull even harder whilst the Alsatian continued to howl. Then, with a final twist and yelp, the dog's paw was suddenly free.

Barney pitched over and was soon soaked through. With one limping bound, the dog leapt over him and jumped out of the broken hatch with a joyful bark. Staggering to his feet, Barney followed while the barge gave another lurch as the water level inside increased. Then he paused. The cap was still floating round the cabin. Instinctively he returned. The water was above his waist now but he grabbed at it and waded back as quickly as he could. Why he had picked it up he didn't know. But it had something to do with his anger.

Standing shivering on the bank, Barney looked down at the hat in his hand. Who did it belong to? Was it a clue to the person who had tried to drown the dog or was it all an accident? Had the barge simply sprung a leak? Then he remembered something. When he had been so desperately groping in the water, he had been able to feel the hole in the decking. It was sharp and fragmented, as if someone had smashed it with an axe. He looked at the cap. There was a dark stain on the crown. Could it be blood, or was there some perfectly simple explanation? Perhaps it was an accident, and he was simply making a drama out of it all. And how was he going to explain away his wet clothes at home?

Barney looked around for the dog but it was nowhere to be seen. Then he heard a snuffling and saw it round the back of one of the dustbins that fronted the barge. He walked over to it and it sat down and stared up at him trustingly. He took the paw in his hand and the dog offered no protest, not even moving as he examined the wound. A long ragged rent had been opened up and the blood was welling out thick and fast. Barney knew that he should somehow get the animal to a vet. But how? He was mentally wrestling with this new problem, squatting down by the dog's side, when he sensed someone behind him. He turned but never saw his assailant as he received a blow on the head that made him see stars and then a long black tunnel yawning in front of him.

The water was coming into his mouth and pouring down his throat. Barney knew he was dreaming as he choked and struggled, but why didn't the dream go away? Why didn't he wake up? His panic grew until he was listening to his own screams. Then he opened his eyes to find himself lying on a bunk with water lapping over his chin. For a moment his panic increased, for Barney was certain that he was in some way tied to the bunk. When he realised that he wasn't he rolled off, landing with a splash in the water-filled compartment. He dragged himself towards the broken hatch. His head was splitting and he felt sick.

It was dark when Barney scrambled back on to the deck again. He was shivering violently and as he staggered over the gangplank he slipped and almost fell into the sea. Then he was on dry land again and moving slowly towards the dustbin where the Alsatian had been. There was no sign of him now, and when Barney looked around muzzily for the cap he saw that that too had disappeared.

With increasing nausea and his head throbbing, Barney walked home. He reached up to his scalp and felt a crust of dried blood. Somehow he managed to keep going, but when he finally arrived outside his own front door he was only able to bang at it once before falling to his knees. There was no reply. He struggled up and banged again and again before he saw the sellotaped notice: GONE TO PUB. BACK AT TEN.

Now what was he going to do? Barney crumpled up, and when he tried to rise to his feet again he found he was too weak. He passed out momentarily, and when he looked at his watch he saw that it was just after nine and it had started to rain. Was he going to die here? The shivering began all over again and his wet clothes clung to him. He must have lain there helplessly for about ten minutes when he suddenly caught sight of the light at the bottom of the garden. It was moving to and fro. He shouted again and again but there was no reply. Then the light seemed to hesitate. Barney thought of being shipwrecked. The light looked like a boat. Would it pass him by, or was there a slim chance of rescue? It wavered and then reluctantly it began to head his way.

Chapter Three

It was Alice. She was holding a torch with a powerful beam.

"What the hell are you doing?" Her voice was as hostile as it had been before but Barney had no pride or anger left.

"Help me," he whispered.

She scowled down at him. "Get up."

"I can't."

"Why?"

"I'm wet."

"Don't be an idiot."

"Wet through." Barney was almost in tears. "I've rescued a dog from a barge. It was trapped. Trapped by someone. And I found something and then someone came along and hit me. My head hurts." He began to sob. He looked up at her pleadingly, and was amazed to see that a complete change of expression had come over her face. It was no longer hostile; it was rigid with shock. "What's the matter?" he choked.

"Where's the dog now?"

"I passed out. When I came to it had gone." Still the rain continued to course down. "Why?"

"No reason." She tried to recover but failed. "I just wondered, that's all."

"Do you know about this dog? It was an Alsatian. It was on this barge."

Again a look of shock passed over her face.

"Do you know the dog?" he repeated.

She shook her head quickly. "No. Why should I?"

"I thought you looked as if you did."

"Where are your parents?"

"Down at the pub. At the *Admiral*."

"I'll go and get them," she said abruptly.

"Thanks."

She went away and he tried to drag himself into the shelter of the tiny porch, but it was useless.

Alice seemed to be away for hours but when she returned she was alone. He looked at his watch. She had only been gone ten minutes. Barney gave vent to an enormous sneeze.

"They aren't there," she said brusquely. "Don't they leave out a key for you?"

"They'd expect me to come down to the pub. Do you know what they look like?"

"Yes. I know what they look like."

There was a long silence. The rain was lessening slightly. He gave another sneeze.

"You'll catch your death here," she said grudgingly.

"I'll be all right," he sniffed. "I can't *think* where they've gone."

"You'd better come down our place," Alice said quietly.

"*Your* place?"

"You can come and have a warm-up."

Barney was so surprised by her amazing offer that he just stared at her.

"I can't have you dying out here, can I?" she said with a return to her rough manner. "Can you stand up?"

"I don't think so."

"I'll help you." She was very strong and soon had him on his feet. "Come on, then!" she snapped. "I haven't got all night."

He leant on her all the way down the alley and eventually they reached the cottage. Alice helped him through the fish-smelling hallway and into the untidy living room. It was as uncared for as ever but at least there was a fire burning in the grate, glowing bright and hot, oddly welcoming.

"Sit down on the floor," she said abruptly. "I'll get you some hot chocolate. But you can't stay long."

He nodded and obediently sat down in front of the fire. Suddenly the shabby room was like a haven.

Alice came back quickly with a steaming mug and he clasped it in his hands, sipping at it gratefully. A warm and soaring happiness filled him. Despite his aching head and wet clothes he felt terrific.

"Do you want to –" She paused and for the first time her rough voice had compassion in it. "Do you want a blanket or something? You should get out of those wet clothes."

He found himself nodding obediently again and she went out and returned with a blanket. "I'll be back when you're changed," she said.

Barney stripped off his wringing wet clothes and huddled into the warm blanket. Then he sipped at his chocolate again.

When she returned Alice pulled up the old springless armchair beside him and they sat in a companionable silence, as if they had known each other for a long time. At least that was the impression Barney had. He didn't dare speak in case he said something to destroy the atmosphere.

"Nasty bruise," said Alice finally.

"It's nothing."

"That was Darren, wasn't it?"

"He said I'd broken in here."

"You did come wandering in."

"I'm sorry."

"Can't you stick up for yourself?"

"Well, a bit, I suppose."

Alice looked at him thoughtfully. "That barge," she said.

"Yeah?"

"Did you find anything else on it? Besides the dog?"

"Someone had taken an axe or something to the floor. It's half sunk. Maybe I should have gone to the police."

"Let it be."

"Why?" he said, but his voice was dreamy.

"You poke your nose in too much," she said, but she didn't sound angry. "Anything else you found?" He could feel waves of anxiety coming from her and he wondered why.

"There was a sort of sailing cap. I don't know why but I took it out of the water. I put it down when I was looking at the Alsatian's paw. Then someone clobbered me."

There was a long silence during which Barney could almost feel her tension. What could be the matter with her? She had seemed so sure of herself.

"What's the matter?" he asked.

"Nothing."

Again there was silence but Barney's sense of well-being had now been replaced by a creeping unease. Suddenly Alice rose and went to the window. "They're back."

"Who?" Barney jumped up, startled. He hadn't heard anything.

"Your parents. I can see a light in the window."

"Oh." He was relieved. He had thought she meant her own sinister family.

"You'll have to go," she said in her old abrupt manner.

"Can I see you again?"

"I don't know. It's difficult."

"Why?"

"My father doesn't like strangers. He likes to keep himself to himself." She looked away.

"What do you think about the barge – and what happened?"

"I don't know. It's none of my business. I should forget it."

"Someone hit me on the head."

"You were lucky it wasn't worse. Come on – go home in the blanket if you like. I'll put your clothes in a bag."

Reluctantly Barney stood up and she came over and gently, very gently, pushed his hair aside and looked at the wound.

"It's only surface," she pronounced. "You won't need stitches."

Barney looked at her intently but as she did so the front door was pushed open and they froze as two sets of heavy footsteps tramped through the hall. The door opened. Why hadn't they heard them coming? Barney hoped it was because they had been too intent on each other. The man was short, very dark, with long, greasy hair. He might have been handsome once but his face had caved in, giving him a cadaverous look. Just behind him stood someone much younger, almost a boy. He looked like Alice and his eyes were dull and suspicious.

"Company!" Mr Miller's voice was a surprise. It

was very light, almost caressing. Yet there was no warmth in it at all.

"He fell in the water," Alice said quickly, before Barney could say anything.

"That was careless. There's a lot of it round here."

No one laughed or even smiled.

"He's just going."

"Is that our blanket?" asked her brother. Barney noticed that his voice was similar to his father's, light and expressionless.

"He'll bring it back. Come on, Barney. I'll walk you back."

"Where to?" asked Mr Miller.

"They live up there." She gestured vaguely.

"Neighbours. In the old Browning house."

"That's right."

Barney couldn't help feeling that they were all talking as if they were acting. It was very formal, very stilted. But exhaustion was getting to him now and he was too tired to start analysing anything.

"Let's go," Alice said and she pushed him past the two men. They smelt of distance, of the sea, of wind and waves.

Once they were out in the rain-washed night Alice walked so fast that Barney and his blanket could hardly keep up with her.

"What's the hurry?" he asked.

"I have to get you back. Get them their food."

"Do you do all the cooking?"

"Why shouldn't I?" she snapped. They were at his door now and she turned and abruptly left him.

"When will I see you?" he asked, but she didn't reply.

Chapter Four

"Where have you been?"

That was all Barney could hear as he crossed the threshold. Dimly he saw his parents, both standing, both agitated. His mother seemed close to tears but his father merely looked angry.

Barney didn't exactly pass out – he flopped into a chair and immediately fell fast asleep. It was not until well into the next morning that he woke and found his mother sitting by his bedside.

Slowly, achingly, he sat up.

"How do you feel?"

"Lousy."

"Any sign of a cold?"

"I don't think so." He looked at his watch. "I'm missing school."

"It doesn't matter about that."

"I should go. It'll look as if –" He paused, not wanting to admit what had happened yesterday. But so much had happened. He reached a hand up to his head and found a bandage.

"I put that on last night." She stared at him, hungry for information. "Where did you get to? What on earth's been happening?"

"Alice went to look for you. She said you weren't in the pub."

"Well, we *were*. In the back room. She couldn't have looked very hard. What on earth's been going on?" she repeated.

It was no good – she would have to know. Briefly and with a dry mouth, he told her. When he had finished, his mother closed her eyes.

"We'll have to call the police," she said.

His parents made Barney stay in bed. They felt that his head didn't need any stitches but they weren't satisfied until a Dr James came and pronounced the injury superficial. He was a big, reassuring man with a firm, confident manner and he insisted that Barney stay at home for a least a couple of days.

The policeman who came was a friendly local and he sat down at Barney's bedside with a cheerful grin.

"You been in the wars, son?"

Barney nodded, not knowing what to say.

"Now, you tell me what happened."

He wrote quickly in his notebook as Barney told his story yet again. When it was finished, he said:

"So the missing items are one Alsatian dog, and a sailing cap."

"Yes."

"You'll be pleased to hear they've both been recovered."

"Who by?"

"The owner of the boat. He's very sorry about what happened to you, and grateful to you for rescuing his dog. He wants to see you when you're better."

"Who is he?" asked Barney curiously.

"London bloke. Chap called Kit Mason. He's in advertising or something."

"But what about the damage? To the boat, and to my head?"

"We don't know about that. You obviously disturbed an intruder. Must have been someone with a grudge against him or something. Anyway, he's having the barge repaired –"

"But it wasn't just intruding, was it? Who would do *that* to a dog?"

"Someone who's a nasty piece of work. We're investigating." He stood up. "Nothing you remember about the attack? You're sure you didn't see *anything* of your attacker?"

Barney shook his head. "I told you – he got me from behind. I didn't see anything."

"OK. Now you take things easy. Bangs on the head can flare up later." With that warning he left, and

Barney closed his eyes when his mother came in with a glass of warm milk. She would only ask him what the policeman had said, and what he had said to the policeman, and he just didn't feel up to telling her. And he hated warm milk. Barney pretended to be asleep and, with a sigh, she tiptoed away.

Barney dreamt that he and Alice were in a sailing dinghy off the Whitstable coastline. There was a fresh breeze and the sea was lit by bright sunlight. He had never felt so happy and alive. Alice kept grinning at him. He was at the helm, in command of the situation but not in command of her. She was wild and free – part of the wildness of the sea.

Then there was a roaring in his ears and he saw the same black tunnel that he had plunged into when he had been attacked near the barge. At the end of the tunnel Barney could see himself and Alice in the dinghy. They were being chased by a fast-moving fishing boat, and standing on deck were Alice's father and brother. They were waving their fists, but unlike nightmares they never caught up and the dinghy easily outdistanced them. At other times the dream was different. He and Alice were walking on the marshes, hand in hand. But there was a shadow behind them. And in this case it was gaining. Then he found himself being gently shaken awake.

"Mum?" He sat up, confused and agitated.

"It's all right. Would you like a visitor?"

It was Alice. It had to be. She had come. Barney's face was wreathed in a radiant smile.

"It's a Mr Kit Mason."

"Who?" Disappointment swamped him.

"A Kit Mason. The man who owns the barge. Do you want to see him?"

"OK," said Barney flatly.

Kit Mason was young and trendy looking. He was tall, over six foot, with a tanned face and crinkly hair. He wore a jerkin and very new-looking jeans, and his trainers were sparkling white.

He came and sat down by the bed with complete confidence, as if he was quite used to meeting fourteen-year-old boys who rescued dogs and were banged on the head for their trouble. He offered his hand, lean and muscular. Barney shook it limply.

"Well done!"

"Sorry?"

"Well done!" Kit Mason repeated. "You saved an old friend."

"The Alsatian?"

"Bruno. He's fine."

"What about his foot?"

"Bandaged up by the vet. It was only torn. But if you hadn't come along –"

"It was a horrible thing to do."

"Absolutely."

"Have you any idea who did it?" asked Barney,

almost aggressively, irritated by Mason's bland manner.

"No. Some local with a grudge, perhaps."

"Some grudge!"

"I've only had the barge a few months, and I know someone else wanted it."

"Who?"

"I bought it at an auction. But I sent a bidder. He said someone pushed the bidding up. I just don't know. Maybe the police will find out." He seemed to have passed on all the responsibility to them.

"Was it your hat?"

"No. It was in the barge already."

"I thought it might be an important clue."

"No. But thanks anyway. Look, I'd like to reward you."

"It's OK." Barney felt a sense of anti-climax. So his clue hadn't been important after all.

"No, it's not." He was very firm. "You've been hurt. How about coming out for a sail?"

"In the barge?"

"No." He laughed. "That's just my home. A very waterlogged home now, but I'll soon get it back in shape again. I've already pumped her out and I'll have her repaired in no time. I've got a motor yacht. I'd like to give you a trip. Maybe your parents would like to come too."

"OK." Barney nodded weakly as Kit Mason sprang to his feet, looking rather pleased, as if he'd just signed a contract.

"I'll fix it. Take care!"

He was gone within seconds, leaving Barney feeling exhausted.

That night Barney got up and looked at the Millers' cottage out of his bedroom window. There was a single light; he supposed it was in the living room. Did they never come in till late? They were out all day. What did Alice do on her own? What did she think? Most important, what did she think of him?

Barney continued to watch, hoping she might come out. It was bright moonlight and the cottage with sea and pebbled foreshore behind it was picked out in stark relief. Then, with a start, he saw the figure walking the sea-wall. For a time he could not make out any features. Then he identified that jaunty, confident walk. It was Kit Mason and he was heading straight for the Millers' cottage. When he got there he didn't wait to knock. Without hesitation, he went straight in.

Barney had a very troubled night, his mind tormented by the inexplicable visit Kit Mason had made. He had waited up for some time, but no one had emerged and eventually exhaustion had forced him back to bed. But sleep was impossible and he only dozed until dawn, waking with a grinding headache and the still burning question: what was the link between Mason and Alice Miller? Why had he walked up the front path, and what on earth would they have been talking about? What *did* they have to talk about?

His mother came in at nine with breakfast and Barney forced himself to eat. He was desperate not to spend another frustrating day in bed, however bad he felt.

"I'm getting up," he said, expecting a battle, but to his surprise she agreed.

"It'll do you good."

"What will?"

"We're going out in Kit Mason's boat."

"Great!"

"Sure you're up to it?"

"You bet I am!"

Only she could take a risk like that. That was one of Mum's really good points, Barney thought. She could be vague to the point of neglect. But she could also do amazing things like taking him out in a boat when he was ill or, as she had done in the past, giving him unexpected treats like a Chinese meal for breakfast, a skateboard for an "un-Christmas present" and a visit to Rome on New Year's Eve. She was very unpredictable and the bane of all doctors and school-teachers or any other officials that entered his life.

"We're going at twelve. Have your breakfast and get up slowly."

Barney felt light-headed as they walked down to the harbour. It was a fresh, blustery day and the sea was bright with tumbling green crests. He saw the yacht

44

immediately – sparkling white with sails furled, moving slightly in the sheltered waters. She was called the *Moonstone* and looked brand new. Kit Mason was swaggering down the deck. As usual he was dressed in spotless clothes, rather as if he were on a stage, acting out the part of an amateur sailor.

He was very welcoming as they came aboard, greeting Barney like an old friend and his parents as respected invalids. He settled them in the well of the deck on cushioned seats, and then turned to Barney.

"It's going to be quite a blow."

"Good," Barney replied casually, but he felt a rising excitement. Suddenly he remembered the dog. "Where's Bruno?"

"I left him with some friends. You crew – I'll helm," he said, dismissing the subject of Bruno.

"I don't know what to do."

"You soon will."

The next half hour was a turmoil of flapping sails and then glorious, gusting speed, for once they were out of the harbour it was as if they were flying on waves and wind. Kit Mason was no weekend sailor. He was wholly in command of his ship, handling it as if it were a flying horse. Barney's parents looked terrified but he felt great. It was wonderful to be lashing along like this, the spray on his face, the salt on his tongue. He soon learned what to do with the jib sail and even when he made mistakes Kit never admonished him but laughed, did something about it and then told him what he had done wrong. He was the ideal instructor. Even so, Barney kept wondering

45

what he had been doing in the Miller cottage, but knew he hadn't the courage to ask him.

Later on the wind dropped a little and then almost died away completely. They had lunch on deck: a mushroom and chicken pie, salad and new potatoes. Barney couldn't get enough of it; he hadn't realised how hungry he was. He was also feeling considerably better. Good old Mum! he thought. She's always right about cures. Now the wind had dropped, his parents had cheered up and were telling Kit all about the book they were illustrating. He listened attentively as they rode at anchor about half a mile off shore.

During the afternoon, they sailed close to the Isle of Sheppey, a low, flat, bleak expanse of fields, sheep and the odd building. As they neared the shore they rounded a corner of the island. On the beach was a small, top-heavy looking ship, listing at a crazy angle. Her name, the *Rose*, was carved in large nautical letters on her prow.

"She was blown on to the beach there last night, apparently," said Kit. There was something odd about his expression, thought Barney. Something strained. "They'll probably try to refloat her on the next tide."

Barney could see there was a tug standing by about a quarter of a mile off shore. A man was standing on the deck of the stranded vessel, looking out gloomily.

"What kind of ship is she?"

"Coaster. Only a small one. It was quite a sea last night."

"Will they get her off?" asked his father doubtfully. "She's a long way up."

"I don't know." Kit seemed to lose interest. "Do you want to tie up at the jetty for half an hour? I just want to tinker with the engine for a bit." He sounded slightly impatient.

"Is something wrong with it?" asked Mr Hampton anxiously.

"No. It's just running a bit fast." The impatience was still there and Barney had the feeling that quite suddenly Kit Mason wanted to be on his own.

"Can I explore?" asked Barney.

"Sure. But don't go near the coaster. That mud it's on is treacherous. Almost like quicksand." His voice was friendlier now, concerned.

"I'll be careful."

"You'd better be," said Mr Hampton. "After all you've been up to."

Barney leapt on to the quayside, feeling better for the sea air and the food. All his former muzziness had gone and he wanted to explore. He too wanted to be on his own for a bit. He wanted to think about Alice, to imagine that she was with him and to wonder again and again what Kit Mason had been doing in the Miller cottage and why he had been so peculiar about the coaster. Or was it all his own imagination? Maybe he had dreamt that Mason had walked up Alice Miller's overgrown front path.

The foreshore of the island was made up of little one-track concrete roads, hedges and, behind them, great open fields like prairies. The trees were stunted, blown in one direction, and Barney could see gulls following a tractor over endless ploughed furrows. It was a bleak island. He walked on, suddenly sad.

The ground rose higher as he walked, and when he looked back he could see the stranded coaster, leaning towards the sea. There was an animal moving to and fro on its upturned deck. Barney could just make it out. It was an Alsatian.

He stared at it for some time. Its colour was indistinct. Could it be Kit's Alsatian, or another? It was pacing round the deck, looking at something on the beach that he couldn't see. Then it crouched down, still staring. Barney fancied that the dog was snarling. He watched, fascinated. The Alsatian ran to the lower decks of the listing coaster and began to bark. Something, somebody, must be on the beach. The dog continued to crouch and bark. The sound was oddly precise in the silence of the late afternoon when even the tractor sounded indistinct. Suddenly he saw the Alsatian gather itself together and jump off the side of the coaster, its bark more insistent than ever.

It's probably just chasing a rabbit or something, thought Barney. He walked on, still not wanting to go back to the ship, when he heard another sound. It was a sort of chattering, giggling sound that rose and fell with an almost musical quality – a cross between a distorted transistor and a tape running too fast. It was weird, chilling, and seemed to come vaguely from the direction of the beach or perhaps the coaster. He couldn't really work out which. Then it stopped as abruptly as it had started and the silence seemed to intensify. The Alsatian's barking had ceased and even the far-off drone of the tractor could no longer be heard. He walked on, feeling very uneasy, until the concrete road widened a little. An orchard ran down towards the sea. Through the trees he could see someone running. After a while he realised it was Alice, and a few metres behind her, his jaws fixed in a silent snarl, ran Bruno. There was no mistaking it now. The dog had a bandaged paw.

"Alice!"

She was running blindly, her eyes wide with terror. Barney could hear the dog's growling now, deep-throated and menacing. Then she saw him, and to his joy her whole face lit up. But immediately his pleasure was replaced by a sharp, rising fear. The Alsatian had foam at its lips and it was gaining on Alice. Instinctively picking up a large stone, Barney leapt over the wall and ran down towards her.

Her face was grey with exhaustion and her chest heaving.

"Get behind me!" Barney yelled. He raised the stone and started shouting at the dog. Still it came on, the growling deeper and more menacing than before. Somehow, Alice managed to reach him.

"Go on – keep running! I'll hold him off!" Then Barney saw the old concrete pill-box, half covered in foliage. "Get in there!"

"Where?" She stared at him helplessly, all her tough arrogance gone.

"There, you idiot!" he screamed at her. She saw what he meant and changed direction, but so did the Alsatian.

Barney raised the stone as high as he could, bellowing at the dog and putting himself between it and the pill-box.

"Go on – get off! Go away – get the hell out of it!" The dog hesitated. "Go on! Get out!" He threw the stone over the dog's head and then picked up another. He threw that, but nearer the panting animal. The growl lessened. Barney picked up a handful of stones this time and lobbed them, managing to land most of them very near the dog. He also kept shouting ferociously, but no one came out of the shuttered landscape to help. Then the growling stopped and the Alsatian put its tail between its legs and ran off, followed by a hail of stones from Barney. Soon all he could see was the flash of white bandage amongst the gnarled and windblown apple trees. It had gone. He had beaten it and Barney stood shaking with relief.

He turned back to the pill-box and saw her standing at the entrance, her chest heaving still.

"I've never run so fast," she gasped. "Never." She looked up at him. "Thanks – I don't know how you did that. It's out of control. Dangerous."

"It's the dog from the barge," he replied flatly.

"Was it? I've never seen it before." Alice seemed to stress the words very defensively. He wondered why. Then he wondered why she was here at all.

"What are you doing here?" Barney asked her gently.

"I came to see some friends."

"Where?"

"Here on the island." She gestured vaguely. "Up there."

"How did you get here?"

"My dad brought me. In the boat. We landed the other side."

"I thought you never went out."

"You don't know what I do!" she flashed back. Barney had the very strong feeling she was lying.

The wind was getting up again, whining across the barren landscape.

"Where are your friends?"

She gestured vaguely again.

"You said the other way last time."

"Mind your own business!" she snapped, and there was an awkward silence. Then she repented. "I'm sorry. I'm grateful – really I am. I was just having a look at that beached coaster and that thing jumped off the deck and chased me up here. I thought he was going to kill me. I've never run so fast in my life."

"Maybe it was guarding the ship," said Barney. They stared at each other uneasily and there was an awkward silence. "I came out with Kit," he added.

"Who?"

"Kit Mason."

"Never heard of him."

51

"He's the bloke who owns the barge. He came to see me. That was his dog."

"Then why was it on the coaster?"

"I don't know. Why did he come and see you last night?"

"The dog?"

"Kit Mason."

"He didn't. Are you barmy?"

"I saw him. He walked up the path and went straight inside."

"Rubbish. No one came last night."

"I *saw* him. From the bedroom window."

"Why are you always spying on me?"

"I'm not. I'm trying to help you." They were both angry now, standing a few centimetres away from each other, eyes cold with fury. "Like protecting you from dangerous dogs."

"I told you I was grateful!" she yelled.

"You certainly show it."

"Now leave me alone. You can't buy me, you know."

Barney looked at her in genuine surprise. "I'm not trying to."

"I've got to go."

"Where?"

"Will you *stop* asking me questions!"

"I'm not letting you go." Barney was very determined.

"What?"

"I *said* I'm not letting you go."

"You're not my keeper."

"There's a dangerous dog at large."

She was silent. "All right. I'll skip seeing my friends."

"Where did you say they were?"

"Shut up!"

"I'll walk you back to your father's boat. If it's still there."

"It will be," she said sullenly.

"Which way?"

"Coast path."

Alice set off in front of him. The adrenalin was flowing in his veins and at last he felt he had the courage to ask her the question that had been burning inside him for so long.

"I want us to be friends," he said. "We can be friends, can't we?"

"You go a funny way about it."

"Alsatians?"

"You can't blackmail me into friendship."

"I'm sorry. I didn't mean to."

"We can't be friends." There was a terrible finality in her voice.

"Why?" He knew he sounded plaintive.

"My dad doesn't want me to. It's nothing personal."

"He can't keep you a prisoner."

"He's not. It's my choice. I have to look after him and Jamie."

"There's room for me."

"There's room for no one."

They had arrived at part of the shore that was

screened from the coaster by some derelict farm buildings. Moored to a jetty, Barney could see a small, snub-nosed fishing boat.

"That's it."

"What's she called?"

"*Charm.*"

"That's nice." He must keep her talking somehow. Barney looked round him. There was no sign of the Alsatian. He suddenly remembered its name – Bruno. That made it sound less sinister, but he still remembered those salivating jaws.

"I have to go."

"I'll walk you down to the boat."

"No."

"Why?"

"You know why."

"What about the dog?"

"It's gone."

"It could be lurking somewhere." Barney was desperate.

"No." Her voice quavered suddenly. "But you stay here. Any sign of it, you can reach me."

"I'd rather –" he began, but she turned and kissed him lightly on the cheek. He reeled back in surprise and she was off, running down the narrow path to the jetty without a wave or a backward glance.

"Bruno was on that coaster."

Kit Mason looked up from the engine, his hands covered in oil. Barney could hear his father snoring in the cabin. He looked searchingly into Kit Mason's eyes. Was he going to make it up as he went along? But they were quite steady and he answered casually.

"Damn! Did he get on there? Is he OK?"

"He was chasing Alice Miller."

"Who's that?"

"The fisherman's daughter. Lives at the bottom of our garden."

"He's only frisky. I hope she wasn't frightened."

"She was terrified. He was foaming and growling."

"I *am* sorry. He wouldn't harm a fly."

Barney looked at him in bewilderment. The trouble was that he sounded so completely convincing. "Well, he looked as if he might."

"Yes? Is she all right?" His voice was brisk.

"I took her back to her dad. He brought her over on his fishing boat. She was going to visit friends here." Now he sounded as if he were making a defensive explanation. It was ridiculous, and terribly frustrating.

"Anyway, I'm sorry about Bruno."

"What's he doing here?"

"I lent him to a fishing chum of mine. He's very fond of him. His boat's probably round the other side." His voice was calm, controlled. There was no hint of any agitation. "Trouble is, he lets Bruno have the run of this bit of the island. He'd probably forgotten about the coaster. I'll have to tell him that if he wants Bruno's company he'll have to supervise him better."

"Right." Barney didn't know what else to say.

"Your parents are having a kip, and I've fixed the engine. Runs much sweeter now."

"Good."

"Wind's up again. We'll have a good beat back to harbour."

"Great."

"You're a good crew, Barney."

In spite of everything, Barney found himself glowing with pride. Then he pulled himself together. Kit was not all he seemed. And he was determined to find out why.

The sail back to the harbour was even more exciting than the outward journey. They tacked up and down the estuary, spray lashing their faces, and Barney felt more of a bonding with Kit. His parents were ill, whey-faced in the cabin, but here he was up in the cockpit with Kit, braving the elements and beating them. In the physical euphoria, his suspicions and questions diminished.

Eventually they beat their way into the harbour, exhausted, exhilarated and marvelling at the calm shelter. The wind howled outside the walls, but inside there was sanctuary.

"You folks OK?" asked Kit, with a wink at Barney, welding him into a conspiracy. Barney's parents staggered out of the cabin, green in the face, looking as if they had been relieved from a long, arduous battle. As he helped them up the slimy steps to welcome dry land, Kit said: "You'll soon get your sea legs." Then he turned to Barney. "Well, when you coming out again, then?"

Barney had nothing to say; he was too full of pride. It was not until he was at home and brewing strong tea for his prostrate parents that the unanswered questions returned. And what about the chattering, singing sound he had heard? What on earth was that?

Chapter Five

The next morning he found out. Or at least he
realised he wasn't the only person to have heard it.
Leafing through the local paper, Barney's eye was
caught by the headline: THE SONG OF THE
DEAD. Reading on, he felt a chill steal over him.

The old Whitstable graveyard legend is abroad
again. Various local residents have claimed to have
heard "the song of the dead" over the last few days,
drifting from sea to shore. This strange sound,
possibly caused by freak weather conditions with
wind striking shore, has not been heard since 1946
when similar phenomena were reported. The
legend began in the early twenties, when the crew
of a foundered Thames barge were washed up near
Island Wall and were buried in St. Thomas's

graveyard. The next day their graves were found open with piles of fresh earth scattered for many metres around. It was as if the bodies had hurled off the suffocating earth and escaped into the sea, back towards the sunken barge. They were to be heard chattering and singing for weeks afterwards, somewhere offshore.

"I heard that," Barney told his father, who was sitting up in bed, gripping his early morning cup of tea as if his life depended on it. Beside him his wife slept on, grasping her pillow as if to emphasise her anxiety to remain on dry land.

"Mmm?"

"I heard that sound – the song of the dead."

"What rubbish are you talking about?" His father was very definitely out of sorts. He read the article irritably. "Nonsense!"

"It was just like it. Near that beached coaster."

"There's probably a natural explanation. There always is."

"Dad –"

"Now shut up and go away. What *is* today?"

"Thursday."

"You can go back to school tomorrow."

"OK." Barney didn't look very keen.

"Oh, and by the way, remind me never to go sailing again. It's lethal."

Sitting in his room, Barney thought about the sound and the newspaper article. Of course there must be some kind of natural explanation as the journalist had suggested. Of course it must have been caused by the weather. It was one of those extraordinary sounds for which, in the end, there was a boring reason, and once it was explained everybody would be smug about it. As it was, he remembered the strangeness of the sound and shuddered. But his memory did not bother him long, for just as he was staring blankly out of the window he saw Alice. She was running up the alley towards him, her hair flying in a wind that was, if anything, stronger than yesterday. But it was her face that appalled him. It was twisted with emotion and tears were flooding down her cheeks. He opened the door before she could knock, and she practically fell into his arms.

"They're missing!" she gasped.

"What?"

"Dad and Jamie. They've found *Charm*. She was upside-down." She finished the sentence on a shrill, terrible cry.

"They were –"

"They went night fishing. Barney, what am I going to *do*?" She was so distraught that she could hardly stand up.

"Come in," he said inadequately.

"No. I'm going down to the harbour to see if there's any news. I want you to – to come with me."

Barney felt a tremendous jolt of emotion. After all that had happened, she needed him. It was like a miracle and he was determined not to let her down. Then his wild elation was replaced by guilt. However badly her family treated her, they were all she had. And now they were missing.

"Of course I will." He grabbed a coat, yelled up to his father that he was going out and probably wouldn't be back for a while, and banged the door behind him. She was half running as they hurried towards the harbour and he had a job keeping up with her.

"They shouldn't have gone," she panted.

"Night fishing?"

"They weren't fishing. Oh, God! They weren't fishing."

"Then what *were* they doing?"

"What?"

"What *were* they doing?"

"Nothing. They were fishing. I told you – night fishing."

"Alice. Tell me what's up."

"They're missing, you idiot! They're missing. He's got them. Oh, God, he's got them!"

"I don't know what you're on about."

She was sobbing now, so hard that she could hardly catch her breath.

"Stop!"

"No. There might be some news."

"Tell me what you're on about. Who's *he*?"

"I'll tell you at the harbour."

They both ran now and arrived five minutes later, out of breath. Even Barney was dreading what they might hear. An anxious group of men stood by the water, talking softly. Directly they saw her, one of them came up and put his arms round Alice.

"No news yet, love."

She just stood there, staring.

"Better get home and wait. No sense in hanging around here. They're searching with helicopters and boats. Air Sea Rescue are doing all they can."

"I'm staying here."

"I'll ring you. Like I did this morning."

"I told you. I'm staying here."

"OK love." The man was middle-aged, avuncular. He let her go gently.

"Come and sit over here on these nets," said Barney. She obediently followed him and then sat down, still shaking. "They're going to be all right," he said hopefully, trying to be reassuring. But Alice was impatient.

"Don't be a fool!"

"They've got a life-raft. I'm sure they'd –"

"Shut up!"

They sat silently for a while. Then Barney said: "What were you saying? About him getting them. And –"

"I told you to shut up!"

"If you tell me it'll help."

"No. Things are bad enough."

"Share it."

"Get lost!"

She stared miserably out at the group of men, as if she were willing something to happen.

"They're all I've got," she muttered. "They're all I've got."

He risked putting his arm round her, and found to his relief that she didn't push it away.

"Let me help you."

"What can *you* do?"

"Listen."

"To what?"

"There's something happening here. Is it to do with Kit?"

"Kit who?"

"Don't start that again." He was impatient now.

"I don't understand."

"You *do*. But you're afraid to tell me."

He was suddenly conscious that her whole body had gone rigid. Barney looked up to see a man he vaguely recognised standing over them. Then he remembered. It was the Dr James who had come to see him a few days before. He looked solid and reassuring, as if he wouldn't allow death to happen.

"Alice. I've heard."

She nodded miserably, if anything even more tense.

"There's hope. They're still searching." Dr James' voice was steady and confident.

"They're dead," she said. "I know they're dead." Her voice was dull, but when Barney glanced at her he saw with surprise that she was looking up at Dr James with hatred in her eyes.

"I remember you," said Dr James to Barney, not seeming to notice Alice's malevolent gaze. "You were the boy mixed up in that barge business."

"Yes."

"How are you?"

"Much better."

"Good." He took Alice's hand and she froze. "Would you like me to wait with you for a while?"

"I'm fine."

They were interrupted by a fisherman with a walkie-talkie.

"Alice!"

"Yes?" She jumped to her feet.

"They've found your dad. He's alive."

She gave a little broken cry of joy and clung on to Barney's arm. But Barney was looking at Dr James. For a moment his air of confidence had disappeared. Instead he looked afraid, very afraid. But the expression was gone in a second as his face lit up with a smile of pleasure. Maybe it's me, thought Barney disconsolately. Maybe I'm imagining things. Alice's hatred; Dr James's fear – they were probably both figments of his imagination.

"Thank God!" said Dr James fervently, and Barney was jerked sharply back into the present. He put his arm round Alice protectively and she nestled against him again.

"That's great," he whispered.

"They're bringing him in now," said the fisherman.

They looked beyond the harbour entrance and saw a small trawler motoring at full speed. Its wake streamed out as a broken silver band and dozens of seagulls followed, wheeling and mewing in the salty air like a crowd of revellers pursuing a wedding party.

It was a brave sight and Barney suddenly realised how close the fishing community was. They were bringing home one of their own.

"I'll stay and meet them," said Dr James. "I'll just go and arrange for an ambulance." He hurried away as the triumphant fishing boat drew closer, watched eagerly by the crowd on the quayside.

Mr Miller was alive, but only just, Dr James explained as he drove Alice and Barney to the hospital.

"He's swallowed a lot of water and he's got severe concussion. If they can stop him developing pneumonia, they can save him." He was frank and confiding as if he were talking to grown-ups.

"What about Jamie?" Alice kept asking, but Dr James only said:

"I'm sure they'll pick him up." He sounded briskly reassuring, but clearly Alice was not convinced and by the time they reached the hospital, Barney could see that she had worked herself into an agony of despair.

"It'll be all right," he whispered, squeezing her hand.

Angrily she shook herself free. "Why do you talk rubbish?" she hissed.

Barney withdrew into himself, feeling inadequate, and said nothing – dared to say nothing – for the rest of the journey.

When they arrived at the grey box of a hospital,

Alice seemed to go to pieces. She walked slowly towards the entrance, head down, her hands clenching and unclenching. He tried to put his arm round her again but she shook him off as violently as before. He heard her muttering, "I'm going to be alone – I'm going to be alone. Always." His heart bled for her.

"Will you come in and wait with me?"

"Do you really want me to?"

"You *must*."

"OK, then." Barney was amazed at the sudden change in her. Dr James passed them on to a staff nurse and then hurried away "to see another patient", he had said. The nurse was sympathetic, but only said Mr Miller was "very poorly".

They sat in the corridor, hunched up and dejected. Eventually the nurse said Alice could see her father, but only if she was very quiet and didn't upset him.

"Your friend can wait for you here," said the nurse authoritatively.

"He's coming with me."

"I'm afraid that's impossible." The nurse's lips were clamped together in sudden determined disapproval.

"Why?" Alice was instantly aggressive.

"Only next of kin."

"He's coming."

"I'm afraid –"

"He's my cousin."

"Oh –" The nurse hesitated and then gave in. Barney reckoned she didn't like the look in Alice's eyes. "Very well, then. But you mustn't be long."

"Will he die?" Alice's voice trembled and the nurse looked at her with compassion for the first time.

"We think he'll pull through," she replied gently.

"Alice?"

He was propped up with a hard-looking pillow. His face was bruised, there was a cut over his eye and he was breathing with difficulty.

"Dad –" She stood beside him hesitantly, while Barney sat awkwardly on a chair against the wall.

The staff nurse said quietly, "You can touch him."

Alice stroked her father's face and he half-smiled.

"I'll leave you with him, just for a few minutes." The nurse left and the atmosphere immediately changed from uncertainty to rejoicing.

"You're alive!" she whispered.

"Just." His voice seemed muffled, as if the water he had swallowed were still there. "He almost did for me."

"Who?" Her voice was hard, very distinct.

"Can't talk now. Where's Jamie?"

"They're looking for him," Alice faltered. She had no instructions. What should she say?

"He's got him then. I hoped he'd taken him." His voice trailed away and Mr Miller closed his eyes. He mumbled something and then became clearer again.

"It's got out of hand. Right out of hand. I never expected this." He was muttering and tossing his head from side to side.

Alice took his hand and Barney felt himself go rigid with tension. There was some unspoken threat in the air, something that she had been living with and he hadn't. And because he had no idea what it was, it seemed all the more unnerving. He was sure he was right now, that he was not imagining anything.

Mr Miller continued to shake his head, still muttering incomprehensibly. Then his words suddenly became clearer. "He'll be on the *Rose* – that's where he'll be. He'll – have taken him there. So he can't say nothing. Not till the day –"

"Dad, was he with you? Out there. In *our* boat?"

"It was rough. They came alongside and boarded."

"What in?" she whispered urgently. "What kind of boat were they in?"

"Looked like fishermen –" But his unexpected clarity was breaking up again and he lapsed into a jumble of slurred words. "Boarded – took an axe to her," were the only words Barney could hear. But they were enough. Whoever they were, their axe had featured before. If they had taken an axe to the barge, an axe to the *Charm*, where would they strike next?

"What's going on?"

They were standing in the foyer of the hospital while people bustled purposefully around them.

Barney felt as if they were on the island again, their own isolated island in the middle of turmoil.

"What do you mean?" she said absently.

"You *have* to tell me if I'm to help you."

"Who wants you to help me?"

"*You do*," said Barney boldly.

She was silent. Then she said, "How do I know I can trust you?"

"Try me."

"How do I know you won't blab to your parents?"

"Try me."

She suddenly produced a grin. It disappeared immediately, but it was a relief. "OK."

"Go on then," said Barney encouragingly as she seemed to hesitate.

"We were being paid by Kit."

"What to do?"

"Help him out," she said obscurely.

"What with?"

"He wanted us to pick something up in the *Rose* and then moor her out by the island. They were to stay on the *Rose* until he's ready."

"Ready for what?"

"I can't tell you. That's Kit's business."

"Was it legal?" asked Barney.

"I don't know. It was brave."

"Of who?"

"Kit."

"And you?"

"It was Dad and Jamie. They didn't have to be that brave. Anyway, Dad blew it. As usual."

"How?"

"He was drunk, wasn't he? He piled the *Rose* up."

"You mean the coaster on the island? The wrecked one?"

"Kit was furious. They were stranded, making a racket."

"Who was making a racket?"

She grinned and then frowned. "You're not having me that way. I'm not betraying Kit. I'll only tell you our part, not his."

"*I'll* not betray him. I've been out sailing with him," said Barney indignantly.

"I can't take any risks."

"If you don't give me the whole picture –" Barney's voice petered out. "Anyway, who sunk your boat? Kit Mason?"

She shook her head angrily. "Of course not."

"Then who?"

"Dr James," she said quietly.

"You're joking?"

"No."

Barney stared at her in amazement. "Dr James? He's – a doctor," he said inadequately, his mind racing.

She laughed scornfully. "He wouldn't have done it personally, but I'm sure it was him. Sure."

"But *why*? Why should he do it?"

Alice hesitated and then shook her head. "He was

70

desperate, I suppose. Trying to warn us off." She paused as if trying to make up her mind. Then she said, "I just can't say any more. I know it's rotten, but I can't take the risk. It's all out of control already." She seemed genuinely sorry this time and even took his arm. "Look, Barney, I *do* want your help. But I can't give Kit away, not even if you make a million promises and I'd known you forever. There's too much at stake for him. But I'll tell you one thing –"

"Yes?"

"He's a good man and a brave man. He's standing up for something."

"And you won't tell me what."

"I can't. Don't pester me."

"All right." But Barney couldn't resist asking, "Did Dr James wreck the barge then? And trap Bruno?"

Alice nodded. "He paid someone to do it, someone who's – who's really dangerous. Dr James, he's just panicked his way through it all. And now he's really blown it." She looked at him intently. "You don't believe me, do you?" she added.

"I don't know what to believe."

They were silent.

"What now?" asked Barney, wondering how much longer they were going to stand in the foyer.

"I said I needed your help. Have I got it?" Alice was once more resolute.

"You know you have."

"Even if you don't really understand what's going on?"

"Even then," he said reluctantly.

"We're going to the *Rose*."

"To –"

"To rescue Jamie."

"You think he's there?" Barney sounded doubtful.

"He's *got* to be. He can't be drowned." Her voice broke pitifully, but then she added, as if to reassure herself, "Dad *knows* he's on board."

"Why should they be holding him?"

"Because they reckon he'll give the game away before they're ready."

"Before Kit's ready?"

She didn't answer.

"Look, if he's such a nice brave guy, why's he kidnapped your brother?"

"Because he rescued him, not kidnapped him. And now he's holding him for his own good."

"But –" He was sure Alice was making it all up as she went along in a blind determination to convince herself that her brother was still alive.

"Because Jamie can't be trusted."

"So why are we rescuing him?"

"Before Dr James gets there. He can harm them all, Kit and Jamie and everyone else on board."

Barney shook his head. Of all the villains in the world, the reassuring, concerned Dr James was surely the most unlikely.

"He's evil," said Alice quietly. "You should see what he did to them."

"Them?"

"Barney, will you promise me something?"

"If I can."

"Help me. But don't ask any more questions. Do you promise?"

"Yes," said Barney sadly. "I promise." He had never felt so curious or so frustrated in his life.

"Let's go then."

They hurried across the foyer and over to the swing doors, hardly noticing the huddled group of men. Then one of them turned sharply.

"How is he?" It was Dr James.

Alice's look of terror almost convinced Barney. "Fine. I mean better. He talked a lot," she said in confusion.

"Did he?"

It was just impossible to believe in him as a villain, thought Barney. He was the average family doctor: calm, anxious to be helpful, yet with an an underlying authority and confidence. Absolutely in control.

"Yes –" Alice's terror was now buried deep inside her, yet understood by Barney. But surely she must be mistaken in some amazing way.

"I'll run you home," he said cheerfully. The kind note in his voice seemed absolutely genuine.

"We can get a taxi." Alice's voice was tense.

"I wouldn't hear of it," replied Dr James. "Come on, now – it's getting late."

The drive was as reassuring as Barney had expected. Dr James talked sympathetically about Mr Miller, but finding Alice given to one-word answers, he turned to Barney, who was sitting in the front.

"So you're holidaying here, are you?" he asked jovially.

Barney began to explain and luckily the explanation lasted most of the way home.

"Shall I drop you at your doors?" asked Dr James.

"No," said Alice. "We'll get out by the harbour."

"Isn't it getting a bit late? It's been a really long day for you both," insisted Dr James.

"We shan't be long," said Barney. "We both need a bit of fresh air."

"It's after nine."

"We'll be home by half past," persisted Barney, and that seemed to satisfy him. He let them out with a hearty goodnight and a soft message of hope to Alice.

"There you are. What did I say?" she said immediately he had driven away.

"Well, he doesn't exactly look like an arch villain, does he?"

"You'd understand if you knew what he did."

"I *do* know. He's a GP."

"I mean if you knew what he *really* did."

"If you'd tell me I'd understand," Barney snapped, suddenly feeling tired.

"Are you going to help me or not?" Equally suddenly, Alice was helpless again and her voice had a pitiful note to it.

"Of course I am." Barney took her hand. She didn't pull it away but clung to it as hard as she could. "When are we going?"

"Tonight."

Barney hesitated. "You said Jamie wasn't in any danger."

"He will be if Dr James gets there."

"Why should –" Then he remembered about not asking questions. "OK. But I'd better go home, go to bed and then bunk out of the window."

"All right. I'll meet you at eleven. Don't go to sleep."

"As if I would!" replied Barney hotly.

When he got in, Barney found his parents busily engaged in planning one of the book illustrations, and when he said he was tired and was off to bed, they were too engrossed to ask him where he had been or even whether he wanted something to eat.

Once in his bedroom, Barney lay on his bed and looked at his watch. It was just after half past nine. He had an hour and a half to go. He got up and went to the window. Pulling aside the curtains, he stared out into the night. There was a great white full moon with clouds scudding across its waxen face. The sea was very calm, almost still, gently sighing at the shifting pebbles. The huddled clapboard houses, the harbour arm running out to sea like a knobbly finger, the breakwater looming up out of the rising mist – all gave the impression of time suspended. He looked at his watch again; the minute hand had hardly moved. How on earth was he going to keep awake? Desperately, Barney propped his elbows on the windowsill, put his chin in his hands and inhaled deep breaths of chilled night air. He was determined to stay awake. But in a few seconds, despite his uncomfortable position, he was fast asleep.

Chapter Six

"Barney!"

"Eh?"

"Barney! Wake up, you prat!"

"Eh?"

"I said wake up!"

When he came to, Barney saw Alice below him, staring upwards furiously.

"You prat!" she repeated, hissing up at him. 'You must have gone to sleep propped up."

"So –"

"Good thing you were at the window. If you'd been lying on the bed then it –"

"Well, I wasn't."

"Keep your voice down. Your parents asleep?"

"How should I know?" The searing fatigue was

back, twice as painful as before.

"All the lights are out."

"Then they're asleep."

"How you getting down?"

"Drainpipe."

"Then make it snappy."

Suddenly he wanted to yell at her for being so bossy. What kind of lunatic trip was he off on? Rescuing someone who probably didn't want to be rescued, being held by a man who hadn't kidnapped him and whom Alice obviously admired. He felt an unexpected twinge of jealousy for the now mysterious Kit Mason.

"Are you coming?" she hissed impatiently.

"Sure," he grunted, climbing stiffly over the windowsill and grabbing hold of the pipe. For a moment he thought it would come off the wall of the house, but it held and he dropped down lightly beside her.

"Athletic, aren't you?" she said with a grin, and he didn't know whether she was admiring or laughing at him.

"Maybe," he said evasively, still unsure of himself.

"It's a bit of a sail," she said, and Barney suddenly realised what a fool he'd been. He knew the *Rose* was on the island but he'd been too tired to think how they would get there.

"Sail?"

"I've got a dinghy – it's Jamie's."

"There's no wind."

"The tide will take us," she said gently. "And thanks for coming."

The sail across to Sheppey was quite magical and reminded Barney uncannily of his dream. The little dinghy cruised the smooth water lightly, the current taking it in a semi-circle towards the island. Neither Barney nor Alice said anything but simply sat in a companionable silence. Barney's original agitation had gone and his rather crumpled sleep against the windowsill seemed to have refreshed him enormously. He was almost looking forward to the adventure now and the presence of Alice gave him confidence, for he felt she was far more tough and resolute than he. He knew it was desperation that was driving her on, but she needed him and that gave him a glow of pleasure. But as they came nearer the island, some of his confidence began to seep away.

"Where's the *Rose*?" he asked as they hauled the boat up the muddy beach and made it fast.

"You know – round the corner."

"Anyone on board?"

"Only Kit."

"So he's on his own."

"Oh, yes."

"I've been thinking."

"That's not good for you." He couldn't see her face in the darkness, but he could feel the smile in her voice. "It makes you ask questions."

"Yes, well, I've got one now. If Dr James wanted

to warn you off, he didn't have to go and sink your boat and nearly drown your father. And surely he wouldn't have sunk that barge of Kit's and never cared about the dog inside –"

"All right," Alice spoke reluctantly. "I didn't want to tell you this."

"Why?"

"I thought you might be scared."

"Thanks."

"I told you before. Dr James has made one hell of a mistake, and he employed some people who are animals. I think he thought they'd just warn us off. He never realised how much they love violence – how much they welcome it."

"The fishermen your father mentioned?" said Barney shrewdly.

"Not anyone from here," she said quickly. "Now stop asking questions."

"OK," said Barney. He had advanced a bit further into the mystery and he didn't want to spoil it by making her clam up. Not now. But she seemed to sense what he was feeling and for once tried to be a bit more communicative.

"They're barmy, that lot. They must be. I don't reckon Dr James will use them again. Not after what they done."

"He sounds barmy to have used them in the first place. A local doctor employing a pack of hooligans – it doesn't seem –"

"You're going to ask questions again, any minute. Let's get going."

"OK."

"When we get there, we'll try and board her and see if Jamie's there."

"Can I ask *one* question?"

"No."

"One you may have forgotten."

"What is it?"

"S'pose Bruno's here?"

"The dog? Well, he's OK really. It's just when he's on guard. But you and him are mates, aren't you? After all, you saved his life."

"He may not see it quite like that," said Barney miserably. "He may remember those rocks I threw at him."

"Here we go!" Alice hissed.

The *Rose* was still up on the beach. The tide was out and she looked more of a wreck than ever.

"We're going to board her?"

"How else do we get in?" And she was off, into the darkness, across the mud and swinging herself up on a higher piece of ground. From there, she was on the *Rose* in a few seconds, standing on the prow and signalling Barney to come up.

"Round the back."

"OK."

"Let's go!"

She led him on, round past the wheelhouse and towards a hatch that was half open.

"Here."

There was no sign of Bruno. Maybe there's no one on board at all, Barney hoped. Even Jamie. But if Jamie wasn't on board, where was he? Drowned? He hoped for Alice's sake he wasn't. They squeezed through the open hatch to a hold which smelt strongly of fish. It was empty but there was a bulkhead and another hatch. Trying to take the initiative, Barney pulled at it, but it wouldn't move.

"Try again," she whispered.

He tried but it was stuck fast.

"Let me." She pulled with all her might and it came with a rush and what seemed like an awful lot of noise. They stood on the boarding, terrified at what they had done, listening with all their might. But no one came.

"Come on." She disappeared stealthily through the dark space, and Barney followed. It was pitch dark inside, but they could hear something. Barney recognised the sound first. Someone was breathing.

"Who is it?" she whispered. Alice had obviously come to the same conclusion. Barney could have hit her for speaking out, but what else were they to do? Stand here forever? There was no reply.

"Who is it?" she repeated.

This provoked a kind of spluttering sound. Someone was waking up.

"Who's there?"

Barney recognised the voice at once; it was Jamie's rather peculiar light tones.

"It's Alice."

"Alice . . ." There was a click and a dim light

revealed a kind of makeshift cabin. There was no porthole and Jamie was on a mattress with a blanket to cover him. "What are *you* doing here?"

"We've come to rescue you."

"I don't *need* rescuing." He was quite angry.

"You certainly do." Her anger matched his own.

"I'm keeping guard," he said.

"Guard? Do you know what happened to Dad? He was nearly drowned."

"I thought he'd be OK," said Jamie vaguely. "He's a good swimmer."

"How did you get here?" asked Barney, sensing that Alice was too furious at Jamie's callousness to speak.

"Swam for it, didn't I? Knew I had to get to Kit. He'd know what to do."

"To do *what*?" asked Alice in a choked voice.

"To get James. What else?"

"And now you're –"

"On guard. Waiting for him."

"You were asleep," said Barney rationally.

"I'd have heard anyone coming on board."

"We got on board." Barney was angry now. Was Jamie lying or what?

"You keep your mouth shut. Both of you. Clear off! Kit and I have sprung a trap, and we don't want you two messing it up."

There was a sudden scrabbling and a weird chattering, keening cry came from somewhere nearby. It was an appallingly frightening sound and Barney felt himself go rigid. Then an ice-cold trickle of fear began to spread down his spine. He had heard the sound before – it was the song of the dead.

"What's that?" he asked.

"You told him?" said Jamie accusingly to Alice.

"No," she said baldly.

Gradually the chilling sound died away, but Barney was still shivering. "What's that?" he repeated.

"Never you mind."

Then they heard another sound. Footsteps on the deck.

The footsteps paused, and they heard the rattle of a lock.

"That'll be Kit," said Jamie with considerable relief, but Alice and Barney stared at each other anxiously, not knowing what their reception would be. Another door opened somewhere in the well of the coaster and the grotesque chattering, singing sound returned briefly. Then it died away again as the door closed abruptly.

Jamie laughed. "Back in Whitstable, they say it's the song of the dead. If only they knew! Still, it's been a good cover-up."

The door behind Jamie's makeshift bed opened, and standing on the threshold was a dishevelled Kit Mason in oilskins and Wellington boots. His expression changed from a grin to a look of fury as he saw Alice and Barney.

"What the hell are you two doing here?"

Barney was suddenly determined to take the initiative and got in quickly before Alice could speak.

"What the hell are *you* doing with Jamie?" He surprised himself by the strength of his protest and Mason looked slightly taken aback.

"What do they know?" he snapped, turning to Jamie.

"I don't know what Alice has told him."

"Only our part," she said woodenly.

"He shouldn't even know that. You Millers are hopelessly incompetent. First your drunken father piles this coaster up, second he . . ."

"Hold it!" said Jamie angrily. "Watch what you're saying. He could have drowned."

"You haven't explained why Jamie's here. His father think he's dead," said Barney aggressively, determined to force the truth out of someone.

"Rubbish!" said Jamie. "He'll have guessed."

Kit Mason looked from one to the other and his expression of anger and alarm gradually cleared. He went over to Barney and put a hand on his shoulder. "You must think I'm a right villain," he said.

"I don't know what you are," replied Barney dolefully. "No one'll tell me anything."

"He'd better know," said Kit. 'After all, it's going to happen so soon now."

"Unless Dr James puts his spoke in," said Alice suddenly. "Aren't you waiting for him?"

"Yes," said Mason quietly. "We're waiting for him."

"What's going on then?" said Barney patiently.

"It's quite simple, and particularly unpleasant." Kit Mason paused. Then he went on. "I've never been a righter of wrongs, not until now. But I couldn't let them go on suffering." He paused again. "There's another side to our affable local GP. He's director of an animal vivisection unit." He glanced at Barney, seeing how mystified he looked. "That means he allows experiments on animals. Unnecessary, cruel experiments that pretend to be for the advancement of medicine but aren't. They're usually for some commercial reason."

"What commercial reason?" asked Barney.

"New ways of making beauty treatments, things like that. He's been making a lot of money and so have his friends."

"Where do you come in?"

"Well, you know I'm a journalist. The Animal Rights people approached me. They've been having a hell of a bad press recently and they can do without a high profile in all this. They helped me to break into the lab, and we got them out. The whole lot."

"Got what lot out?" demanded Barney, feeling totally confused.

"I'll show you. In a minute. But let me tell you what I'm going to do with them. Saturday is Animal Rights Day. I was going to sail this trawler up the Thames with them all on board. I'd arranged full press coverage until these idiots wrecked the *Rose*. She was badly damaged when they ran her aground, so I'm waiting for another ship to arrive tomorrow, organised by the Animal Rights people. And then we're going to really make our point, and wreck James's career as well."

"How?" Barney was still bewildered.

"You'll see. I'll show you his victims, but we'll have to be quick. We're expecting him."

"What happens when he arrives?" asked Alice.

"I don't know. Depends if he brings his support team. If he does we're in trouble."

"What will he do?" Barney's voice shook slightly.

"Try to get them back. And it's Jamie and me. That's all."

"The Animal Rights people – won't they help you?"

"Low profile. No publicity. No hassle with the police. The bargain was I was on my own. So it's Jamie and me – and Bruno."

"Where's Bruno?"

"I've left him on the towpath. He'll give us the alert." Kit Mason gave Barney a mock punch on the arm. "I'm glad I let you in on all this. You've got some inititaive, you know!"

Barney immediately wished he hadn't.

"Come and have a look at our little friends while there's time. All of you come with me. We'd better keep together." He turned back to Barney. "You know that the locals think our friends are the song of the dead?"

"Jamie told me. What *is* that horrible sound?"

"You'll soon see," said Kit Mason.

Chapter Seven

Mason led them through to another hold. It was empty and also smelt of fish, but there was something else. Something ranker and sharper. He paused at a steel shutter. "Just stand still when you get in," he said. "Then you won't frighten them." He wound the shutter up gently and the sharp smell increased. Barney stopped, standing silently, staring into the gloom. Something moved, something scurried. Then they were silent as well. Whatever they were. Whoever they were.

"I'm going to switch on the light," whispered Mason. "It's very subdued. Come in and move slowly."

Barney glanced at Alice and was reassured to see her standing quite casually. Yet the occasional scurrying movement and the awful rank smell made him feel sick. There was sweat on his forehead and he kept clenching and unclenching his hands. Slowly, Barney forced himself on until he was under the steel shutter and inside the hold. A wan light suddenly flooded the walls, but the floor space and its inhabitants remained dim, insubstantial. Then something shot up into the grey light and for a ghastly moment Barney saw a brown dwarf with hideously long arms and legs. It had a horrible kind of bouncy, clawing run. He cried out, a mixture of scream and groan, as the creature bounded back into the darkness, huddling amongst more of its kind.

"Don't be a fool!" said Alice sharply. "They're only monkeys, for God's sake!"

"What?"

"Monkeys, you twit. Kit saved them from the lab."

Mason switched on another light and the floor area was better illuminated. Yes, she was right. Barney felt a flood of relief. They were monkeys all right. About a dozen of them. Abnormally thin and dirty looking, but monkeys all the same.

"I've been feeding them up," said Mason. "James and his mates had half-starved them. Conducting experiments – I ask you!" But even in his shocked state, Barney wondered if his voice was somehow melodramatic, *too* outraged – as if he were rather self-consciously acting a part. It was very peculiar, but the thought stayed with him.

The monkeys were huddled together now, limbs entwined, making a subdued version of their chattering, whimpering sound.

"You – you got them away from a lab?" stuttered Barney.

"It's over on Ore Creek, in what was an old Victorian house. I whipped in one night with a couple of Animal Rights groups and got them in crates. Tricky task – took us quite a while."

"Wasn't the place guarded?" asked Barney. It just seemed too easy somehow.

"We doped a guard dog. That's all they had."

'And what did you say you were going to do with them?"

"I'm taking them up the Thames the day after tomorrow. Animal Rights Rally. It would have been nice to have had the *Rose*, but Miller beached her. There's going to be the hell of a big repair bill, and –"

"All right," said Jamie. "Don't keep going on about it."

"The Animal Rights people have chartered another trawler. It should be arriving tomorrow afternoon."

The monkeys were still crouched together for mutual protection, staring up hollow-eyed at their visitors.

"And then what happens to the monkeys?" asked Barney.

"They were sold to James by a private zoo. If they're still OK I'll have to get them back into a zoo. But somewhere where they'll be properly cared for."

"And Dr James?"

"He'll be prosecuted. Look at the condition they're in."

Barney looked. They certainly seemed thin and bedraggled.

"And you reckon he's coming here?" asked Alice, unfamiliar in her role as questioner. "We thought he would be. We came to warn Jamie and you."

"Dr James is coming here all right. No doubt with his little gang of thugs. And we're going to have to repel boarders. The four of us and Bruno." Kit Mason stood there for a moment, staring at them all. Then he said: "I *have* to get the monkeys up the Thames. I *have* to." Barney noticed there was now a real note of despair in his voice and the hint of falseness had gone. It was weird. Did he really care so deeply about the monkeys? He had done so much rescuing them and having his home sunk and his dog nearly drowned, as well as bearing the responsibility for the attack on the Millers. He glanced towards Jamie. "And despite everything you'll be in the wheelhouse of the new trawler. You'll share in all the glory."

Jamie looked pleased and proud for the first time since Barney and Alice disturbed his sleep. Then the calm was shattered. Outside Bruno began to bark, and inside the monkeys began to chatter.

"OK," said Kit. "Don't do anything till they come on board."

He patted the pocket of his waterproof coat.

Barney and Jamie knew at once what was in it. They stared at each other incredulously. Alice took longer to realise what was concealed in his pocket but she was far quicker in speaking out.

"You can't!" she said, and Barney noticed that the look of hero worship was no longer in her eyes. It had been replaced by amazement and then anger.

"What?"

"You *can't* have a gun," she said, her disillusion obvious. Barney, despite the tension, felt a flash of pleasure. Mason took some seconds to react. Then he spoke reassuringly.

"It's only to frighten off those thugs."

"I'm not having nothing to do with guns." Jamie's voice was hoarse with alarm.

"It's a precaution," said Mason evenly. "I'm not going to use it. Obviously I'm not." But it was clear that no one believed him.

"That's what they all say," said Alice. "If you're so scared, call the police." She was scoffing at him now, openly contemptuous.

"And be arrested? Technically I stole this lot." He looked down at the monkeys angrily. As if sensing his change of mood they huddled together even more tightly.

"Is it really a protest?" asked Alice. "Is it *just* for the sake of the monkeys, or is it something else?"

But there was no time to reply. Someone was on deck. Heading for the wheelhouse.

Mason put a finger to his lips. The finger was shaking and he seemed to have lost much of his former control. "There's a hatch in the wheelhouse. Let's wait for him to come down it."

They seemed to wait for hours. The footsteps had ceased and there was only the occasional shuffle interspersed by silence. Then, very abruptly, there came the almost explosive sound of the hatch sliding open. Immediately the monkeys began their song.

"Stay there!"

Dr James wheeled round, his large calm face betraying hardly any shock.

"Well, it would seem I have a reception committee," he said smoothly, stepping smartly off the ladder. He wore a long grey overcoat over a suit, white shirt, tie and slightly muddied black shoes. He looked as if he was making his rounds rather than arriving to pick up a bunch of monkeys. "Young Jamie, Alice and Barney. I didn't know that you –"

"You should," said Jamie. "You nearly killed my old man. You know you did."

"Yes, I acted very stupidly in believing that Tommy & Co. would simply be threatening. I was horribly wrong – I should have realised that after the barge – but I'm afraid I was getting desperate. And once I'd made one mistake I promptly made another." He looked at Jamie with real anguish. "I can't tell you how sorry I am about what happened, and I assure you I'll make it up to you and your father."

"You've got a lot to make up," said Jamie, and there was the light of pleasure in his eyes. And you've got a lot to blackmail him with, thought Barney, and when he looked at Alice he knew she was thinking the same thing.

"How could you do those horrible things?" asked Barney. It was unbelievable that this kind, calm man had even met the thugs who had attacked him and holed the barge and *Charm*, yet alone hired them. But despite his amazement he felt cool and collected. Alice's change of heart over Kit Mason had given him added confidence. Also Dr James seemed to be alone. Maybe it was going to be all right after all.

"I've behaved like a fool," said Dr James. His voice shook. "I'm only trying to clear things up now – to minimise the damage." A little pulse was working in his cheek and all his calm had disappeared.

"But why do you conduct experiments on animals?" Barney was more genuinely puzzled now than revolted. "You're a doctor. You help people – heal them." He stared across at the monkeys, still huddled protectively together. "Why would you want to hurt them?"

Dr James, despite his desperation, spoke with conviction: "As a doctor I see so much suffering. Human suffering. And what sickens me particularly is unnecessary death. Experiments with animals can help human beings not to suffer. Will eventually even cure them. And I happen to think animals are not as important as human beings."

"That's where you're wrong," said Jamie bitterly. "It's sick to experiment on animals. They got rights too, you know. Anyway, we've sussed you out. We know you aren't interested in medicine, in really helping anyone. You're in it for the money, aren't you? Like developing new expensive face creams."

For the first time Dr James looked angry, and then surprised. "Who told you that?"

"We know it's true," said Kit Mason quietly.

Dr James looked at him, contempt replacing the anger. "But you *would* say that, wouldn't you?"

"Torturing animals is terrible either way. It's horrible," said Barney. His voice shook as he looked down at the pathetically entwined monkeys.

"I guarantee he's not in medical research," said Kit Mason, ignoring him. "The outfit he works for is purely commercial. As Jamie says, he tortures animals to help with the manufacture of beauty treatments. Now, maybe you could tell us why you're trespassing on my boat."

"Hoping to reason with you. I can tell you I have *nothing* to do with commercial research. That's a lie." All traces of anger and despair had vanished. He was the professional doctor again, counselling some flurried, hysterical patients. It was amazing how he could change so rapidly. He reminded Barney of someone. Then he realised who it was. Of course – Kit Mason. They could both change so much, so quickly. Maybe they're *both* really desperate, he thought.

"And if we hadn't been here?"

"I would have taken the monkeys back. They're my property. I've got a van and crates on the orchard road."

"And your friends too?" sneered Kit.

"There's no one here but me."

"How did you get past Bruno?" asked Barney with sudden urgency. "Have you hurt him?"

"I did exactly what Mr Mason did to our guard dog. I gave him some doped meat. Now he's having a sleep. But he'll be awake in a couple of hours. Bruno is perfectly safe. I don't *hurt* animals. Look at the monkeys – they're unharmed."

"They're thin," said Alice. "Thin and dirty."

"Dirty because they've been held here, and they're naturally thin. That's their body type."

"You *do* hurt animals," Barney insisted. "What about Bruno?"

"I told you. I stupidly employed . . ."

"It's still your responsibility," said Barney.

"But it was not done with my knowledge," repeated Dr James firmly. "Now, Mr Mason, if you'll just hand over my property."

"No chance. It's going on display on Saturday, and so are you and your kind," replied Kit Mason truculently.

"Then you leave me no other option. I shall go to the police."

"Why didn't you in the first place?" asked Barney.

"Because there would be publicity. I've done nothing to be ashamed of with animals. But hiring a set of yobs –" He paused reflectively. "All my life I've taken decisions slowly, professionally and privately. Perhaps too slowly and maybe that's why I never married. But I was so outraged at the theft, at

96

the childish obstruction of genuine science by cranks, of real progress in medical research being sabotaged by idiots, that I didn't think. I blindly hired a kind of human animal. I thought you'd be warned off – all of you."

Barney had never seen Dr James so vehement, as if he were a general trying to rouse the rabble to win a war. For a moment Barney was taken in. His confidence, his warm brown voice, his authoritarian manner all sounded so right, so certain. Until he looked at the monkeys. And then all the high-minded things the doctor had said turned to a bitter taste in his mouth.

"You'll be prosecuted," said Mason. "The barge, the *Charm* – you could end up with a prison sentence."

But Dr James was unmoved. "I suggest you hand over the animals now. You must appreciate that you have also committed crimes – breaking and entering, theft. So why don't we come to an agreement? Hand me back the monkeys and we'll say no more about your stealing them. And I will financially compensate you, and the Millers, for the damage."

Standing a little apart from the others Barney noted their different reactions with interest. Jamie immediately looked interested, Alice scornful and Kit Mason angry.

"I'm making a protest," said Mason sharply.

"And you're also being paid very highly for it," said Dr James softly. There was a long silence during which everyone's eyes swivelled to Mason's face.

"I don't know what you're talking about."

"I'm sorry. I think you do."

"All I've done is purely voluntary." Mason spoke quickly. "It's part of my conscience as a journalist."

"Rubbish!" Dr James smiled. "They're giving you £30,000 for this, and I can prove it."

"I'm sure you can." Was Mason's voice slightly unsteady? Barney couldn't be certain.

"Vivisectionists have their contacts. We keep an eye on the Animal Rights movement. And my sources tell me that you were offered the money and that the only reason you are carrying this out is *for* the money. My sources are very reliable," Dr James said pointedly. "So I'm afraid your conscience wasn't really in it, was it?"

Mason laughed. "I've never heard such nonsense." But Barney wondered if the laugh sounded uneasy.

Dr James smiled. It was strange, thought Barney. It was as if they were both enjoying a joke.

"I tell you I can prove it," he said. "So we've reached a deadlock, haven't we?"

There was a long silence during which Barney watched a strange change come over Kit Mason's face. It seemed to harden. His eyes were no longer warm but hard and bright.

"We should talk this over without the benefit of an audience," Kit Mason said quietly.

"I'd be willing to do that," replied Dr James.

"I think you should know he's got a gun," said Alice evenly.

Kit Mason gave her a contemptuous smile, pulled

out the gun and levelled it at his own head.

"Can't take it any longer!" He grinned and pulled the trigger.

A wave of nausea gripped Barney in a tight band around his stomach, and all his mind could register was wild confusion and a terrible finality.

Chapter Eight

Jamie slumped to the floor as the trigger clicked emptily. Alice rushed to him, kneeling by his side and stroking his forehead. "Jamie –" she wept.

"He's fainted," laughed Kit. "The gun was empty. I only had it to frighten those thugs away."

Barney stared at him, his heart pounding. So it had been a joke! A horrible practical joke! Was he crazy? He looked at Jamie, his face twisted in fear. The monkeys danced around chattering, and Alice muttered: "You idiot, Kit!" over and over again.

"That was a damn silly thing to do," protested Dr James. "He's had a very nasty shock." He walked over to Jamie, took his pulse and then opened his mouth, making sure his tongue was in the right position.

Groaning, Jamie slowly regained consciousness. He looked up at Kit and said: "You're dead!"

Barney looked on in amazement. Things seemed to be running out of control.

"I'm sorry," said Mason. "The gun wasn't loaded." He didn't look in the least ashamed.

"You idiot!" said Jamie groggily.

"Now, Doctor, if you've finished with your patient, shall we take a walk on the beach?"

Dr James looked at Mason with real contempt. "Do you realise what damage you could do behaving like that? This isn't a game, you know."

But Barney wasn't so sure. Maybe Mason saw it all as a game – a cruel game being played for high stakes.

"I said shall we take a walk?" There was a mocking note to Mason's voice.

Dr James shrugged. "Very well, providing Jamie's feeling better."

"I'm fine," said Jamie quickly. "Just fine."

"Don't go!" said Alice unexpectedly.

"Do you think I'm going to murder him?" laughed Kit.

"You might," she replied with quiet sincerity.

"Thank you. I'll be back soon. Meanwhile, you can look after the livestock. I'll leave the shutter up but I wouldn't let them stray about too much if I were you."

"Maybe Dr James does regret making such a mistake, like hiring Tommy or whoever he is," suggested Barney.

"Don't let him fool you," said Jamie. "He only cares about making money. Some doctor!"

"Kit Mason doesn't seem to be any great shakes either," replied Barney. "Do you really think he's being paid all that money to take these monkeys up the Thames?"

"I don't know," said Alice. "But so what if he was?" But she was looking betrayed.

"It makes it different, that's all," replied Barney. "It means he doesn't really care, doesn't it?"

The monkeys were quieter now, not huddling together so much, and one of the smaller ones, with an old man's head and a tiny body, had climbed up on a lobster pot and was staring at them with beady eyes.

"Can we tame them?" asked Alice suddenly. Barney knew she was deliberately changing the subject. Her hero had fallen, and he was glad.

"They're terrified of humans and no wonder," replied Jamie. He got up and walked towards the nearest monkey. It squealed and ran to the back of the hold. "See what I mean? That Dr James has got something to answer for."

"So what do we do now?" asked Jamie. "Wait here?"

"We'll have to," said Alice. "I'm not letting the monkeys out of my sight." She paused and then said, "I never thought he'd have a gun, or be paid for what he did." Her voice broke. "I thought he was a *good* man."

"He's a main-chancer," said Jamie. "Dad and I always knew that; it's only you who fancied him."

"Me?" She was immediately indignant.

"You. You're a kid, that's all."

"Shut your mouth!"

"Don't speak to me like that, baby face!"

"You stupid –" Alice ran up to him and slapped Jamie round the face.

For a moment Barney thought he was going to hit her back. But instead he just grinned and repeated, "You fancied the guy, Alice, and now you've found out what a nerd he is. So just cool off."

Suddenly all the fight went out of her and Alice collapsed on the mattress, burying her face in Jamie's dirty pillow. As she did so, Bruno began to howl from the bank.

"That must be him coming back," said Jamie sullenly. "But why's Bruno howling? I thought he was doped."

"Maybe he's come to."

This time there were two pairs of footsteps on the deck.

"They're coming back together," said Alice, looking up with dark tearstains under her eyes.

The hatch slowly slid open.

It took some time for the shock waves to clear away. Barney felt sick. He couldn't take any more surprises.

"What the hell are *you* doing here?" asked Jamie

belligerently. But there was real fear in his voice. He turned round to Alice. "It's Tommy."

Barney stared up at him. Tommy was in his mid-twenties with a large, round, almost babyish face. His cheeks were pink and his hair receded on a similarly pink forehead. But it was his eyes that were so shocking. They were very small and deep-set, nugget-like. And they hardly seemed to move at all. It was one of the cruellest faces that Barney had ever seen. How could Dr James ever have hired him? Had he been so very desperate?

"Jason here brought us out in his boat. We thought there was something funny going on." Tommy's voice was flat and expressionless.

"You nearly drowned us," said Jamie. "My dad's in hospital and –"

"I don't know what you're talking about," said Tommy listlessly. "It must be a case of mistaken identity. We never touched you." He seemed very confident.

"Funny? What do you mean, funny?" Alice's voice shook. She and Barney exchanged glances. They were in real trouble now. Dr James and Kit Mason might be villains of a kind, but Tommy was something else.

"Yeah. We saw James leaving the harbour, so we followed. Wanted to know what he was doing out at this time of night, didn't we, Jason?"

"What's that got to do with you?" said Barney recklessly, wondering what they would say.

Another head pushed its way into the hatch. The

face was bearded and hostile, yet not as ruthless as Tommy's. "Thought he might like to settle something on us. He owes us a bit, see? And he doesn't seem to want to give us no more jobs, so Tommy and me thought he might want to keep us quiet instead."

"Blackmail him, you mean?" said Jamie.

Tommy grinned. "Something like that." His smile made him look even more vicious.

"You knocked me out," said Barney resentfully. "And you tried to kill Bruno."

"The dog that was lying in a heap on the beach? Looked doped to me. Only just managed to give a howl."

"He *has* been doped," said Alice. "And you would have let him drown on that barge."

"We didn't do nothing to him. He wasn't even in the barge when we bashed the hole in the floor. He must have come back and got trapped. I wouldn't do nothing to a dog, and neither would Jason." He spoke so passionately that Barney almost believed him.

"He *has* been doped – by James," said Alice again.

"That's the funny thing," said Jason.

"What's funny?" asked Jamie impatiently.

"They was walking along together," said Tommy. "So we dived into one of them ditches and watched."

"Well?" Alice was as impatient as her brother.

"They was walking along," continued Tommy. "And they was laughing."

"Laughing?" Barney stared at him in bewilderment. So much had happened in the last hour that he just couldn't take in any more.

"Yeah, laughing and talking as if they was long-lost mates."

"Where were they going?" asked Alice. She sounded as amazed as Barney.

"They weren't going anywhere. Just walking up and down like."

"Tell you what," said Jamie, "I wonder if Dr James has bought Kit off?"

Tommy lowered himself into the cabin, followed by Jason. They both towered over Jamie and looked very threatening. They'd work for anyone, providing they were paid enough, thought Barney. And we've got nothing. He looked back at the monkeys who, surprised by more visitors, had started to huddle together again. He felt sorry for them. After such a long confinement in the lab, their lives were now nothing but a series of unpleasant surprises. Their chattering began again but he was getting used to the eerie sound by now.

"Laughing and joking together?" Alice was cynical. "That means James is buying Kit off."

"I don't believe it," Barney returned, really upset.

"Neither would I a few hours ago. I thought Kit was fantastic when he first came to see us and made the offer. It gave us something worthwhile to do for the first time in our lives." She was talking to Jamie and he was listening quite intently for him. "I was sick of being knocked around by Dad. He made me a servant – didn't care whether I went to school or not, or anywhere else. And neither did you, Jamie," she added accusingly. She seemed to have completely forgotten the existence of Tommy and Jason, however off-putting they were.

"I never touched you," he said hotly.

"Maybe not. But you stood by and watched him. You both made me a servant. Then Kit arrived and asked us to work for him. It made *my* life different, anyway. Saving the animals. Working for something. But he should never have turned to Dad – he was far too unreliable. Look what he did to this trawler."

"All right, all right!" snapped Jamie. "I know Dad's too far gone to cope."

But Tommy interrupted. "We haven't got time to listen to your problems." He turned to Jason. "Looks as if we could be back in a job."

"How's that?" asked Barney boldly.

"S'pose we shift this lot?" He pointed to the monkeys. "Hide 'em somewhere on the island tonight, and make Mason and James pay for 'em?"

"Monkey ransom, eh?" said Jason. "That sounds a good idea."

"You're not touching them," said Barney. He glanced at Alice. She'd be with him. But what about Jamie?

"Now don't let's act too hastily," interrupted Jamie, sitting down on the mattress. "Let's talk this through."

So Jamie is going to be useless, Barney thought, looking at Alice. He knew she was thinking the same thing. If it came to a fight, it was obvious who would win. His thoughts raced at breakneck speed. If he could escape and get to the mainland, who could help? It seemed hopeless. The police would only return the monkeys to the lab. Then he had a fresh idea. His parents could phone the Animal Rights people. Perhaps they would be able to send some help. It was their only chance. But right now escape looked impossible.

"So," said Tommy, "I wonder what we can shove them in?"

"There's a van and crates on the orchard road. Bring 'em in the van, wire up the engine and take them up to the bridge."

"I thought this was an island," protested Barney. Everything seemed to be conspiring against the luckless monkeys.

"It is," said Alice gloomily. "But there's a bridge, though it's a long way round."

Tommy grinned. "Let's get the crates."

Barney walked over to the ladder. "You're not going anywhere," he said, his voice sounding ludicrously weak and feeble. There was a roar of derisive laughter from Tommy and Jason and even Jamie grinned foxily.

Then Alice moved over to Barney's side. "You'll have to shift us both," she said quietly.

Tommy laughed again and Jason brushed his long black hair out of his eyes, went up to Barney and shoved him hard in the chest. It didn't hurt but caught him off balance and he fell in an undignified heap on the floor.

"Leave him alone!" said Alice fiercely. Barney looked up at her. He had never felt so humiliated.

"Now let's get to those –" But Tommy stopped in mid-sentence, his baby-face suddenly looking far less cruel. His mouth hung open slightly and there was an unexpected softness to him as he watched the hatch slide open again and Kit Mason lowering himself down, loose-limbed and athletic. The monkeys chattered but this time more calmly, as if in muttered welcome.

"What the hell's going on? What are you two doing here?"

Has he really sold out to Dr James? wondered Barney as he struggled to his feet. Then he saw Alice's expression. She was looking at Kit Mason with a mixture of loathing and contempt. The hero has definitely fallen, thought Barney again, but this time he didn't feel much pleasure.

Tommy looked worried and Jason uncomfortable. All their hardness seemed to have gone, but even so Barney was sure they could easily have taken him. Perhaps there was something about Mason's casual confidence that had made them feel vulnerable.

"We came to see what was going on," said Tommy feebly.

"You're trespassing," said Mason angrily. "Now get out!"

"You're working with James now?" asked Tommy in a weak attempt at boldness.

"Don't be a damn fool! Of course I'm not. I

suppose you're the thugs who wrecked my barge. I should have the police on you."

"Saw you two having a laugh and a joke," pointed out Jason. "Very matey like."

"Get out!"

"What's the explanation?" asked Alice quietly, her eyes fixed unwaveringly on Mason's face.

"I've got my plans. I don't intend to reveal them now, so you can think the worst if you like. Now if you two don't get off this boat, I'm going to throw you off." He advanced on Tommy who stood his ground at first and then suddenly backed off.

"Don't threaten me," he said. "I could have you for assault."

"It would be a pleasure," said Kit. "Now get up the ladder. You'll find Bruno recovering fast outside, so make your escape now."

Neither Tommy nor Jason seemed inclined to argue and they disappeared as quickly as they had arrived.

"All we have to do now is wait," said Kit. He glanced at the monkeys, who were sitting preening each other contentedly on the floor of the hold. "The Animal Rights group will be bringing up another boat early afternoon, and then we'll set sail for the Thames. Anyone want to come?"

No one spoke. Barney looked at his watch. It was after four. Dawn would be coming soon. He wondered what would happen when his parents found out he wasn't in bed. They would go spare. And what about school?

"I've got to get back," he said.

"I'll go with him." Alice sounded resolute. "We've got the sailing dinghy."

"Sorry," said Kit. "You're not going anywhere."

"What?" Alice stared at him unbelievingly. "You mean you're keeping us here against our will?"

"Kidnapping us?" echoed Barney.

"I didn't trust Jamie, and I don't trust you." Kit Mason was firm. "You'll stay here."

"But my parents!" wailed Barney. "They'll think I've been kidnapped!"

"You have," said Jamie with a laugh.

"Rubbish!" said Kit. "You can phone your parents now if you like, or when they wake up."

"What shall I say to them?"

"Say you'll be back after lunch; that you're safe and well but you can't tell them where you are."

"You could be charged," said Alice furiously.

"I'm in the risk business." Kit gave her one of his charming smiles. "I'm going to get those monkeys up the Thames. Somehow. Don't you realise, this could be one of the biggest coups for Animal Rights in years?"

"You'll still be charged," said Alice, unimpressed. "For kidnapping humans or monkeys or both."

"Maybe I will," said Kit. "But frankly I don't give a damn. It's the cause that counts."

Barney studied him closely. For someone who had

obviously been bought off by Dr James, he was still a very convincing liar.

They tried to sleep. Alice and Jamie succeeded but Barney couldn't. Not lying on the floor. Chilling thoughts of baby-faced Tommy and his blind violence kept entering his mind. Mason might have scared him off, but he was out there somewhere, waiting for the weak and the old.

At last Barney slept lightly and dreamt that he was on the barge. It was full of water and baby-faced Tommy was tying him to a bunk. The water lapped at his chin and Tommy laughed, clapping his hands together in glee like a child.

When he awoke, all thoughts of Tommy and the menace he presented disappeared. He *had* to escape; he must work out a plan. For the next couple of hours he thought desperately and eventually came up with a possibility. There was no doubt whatever that Kit Mason would escort him to the telephone box – he would never be fool enough to let him go on his own. So he had to give him the slip somehow while they were on their way to the telephone, or on the way back. He would run to the dinghy, sail back to Whitstable and raise the alarm. Dr James and Kit Mason's uneasy partnership would be exposed, Tommy and Jason arrested, and the monkeys saved. He would be the hero of the hour. He would be Alice's saviour. It was all very neat.

After going over the details dozens of times in his

mind, Barney began to think about Alice. He was desperate that she should depend on him, and pleased that her dapper hero had bitten the dust. But would she think that he, Barney, was running out on her? And should he leave her to the dubious mercy of Mason, the doubtful support of Jamie, and the looming presence of Tommy and Jason? But how else could he get help? He longed to discuss it with her but she was sleeping so peacefully and he was afraid Jamie would wake and overhear them if they started talking. And Jamie was unpredictable.

The doubts circled his mind as he lay there, numb and exhausted and utterly miserable.

Chapter Nine

At six, Barney climbed up the ladder and knocked at the hatch. Kit Mason was standing guard in the wheelhouse and when he slid it back, he looked bleary and tired and not nearly as confident as he had been a few hours ago. This gave Barney hope.

"I want to phone my parents."

"Now?" Mason's tone was irritable.

"It's six. They'll be up soon."

"OK." He stood back and Barney came up.

"Mornings aren't my thing," said Mason miserably.

"No?" Even better, thought Barney. "How's Bruno?" he added.

"*Much* better. I've had him in, and now he's just gone out for a run. He doesn't seem to have any after-effects."

114

"Great." Barney suddenly realised they had one genuine pleasure in common – Bruno's welfare. It was an odd feeling.

"All right – let's go."

It was a misty grey dawn. The sea was calm and there was no wind. Barney's heart sank. That wouldn't help with getting back to Whitstable. It could take him hours. But maybe the wind would get up. He could only hope and pray that it would.

There was a telephone box up the concrete road and they walked towards it in silence. Once inside, Barney dialled and waited, seemingly for an eternity. Then his father answered.

"Dad –"

"Barney! What the hell are you doing? Where are you? I thought you were in bed."

"Well, I'm not."

"What? How? Where did you –" His father sounded almost comic in his panic.

"I had to go out last night."

"You what?"

"And I can't tell you where I am. But I'm safe and I'll be back soon."

"When?"

"After lunch," said Barney for Mason's benefit at least. He was leaning up against the box, listening to every word he said.

"Are you in trouble, Barney?"

"No, Dad."

"Then what are you up to? What do you think

115

you're playing at? What about school? And what about –"

"Bye, Dad! Home soon." Barney quickly put the phone down. He looked at Mason. Now he had to take his chance.

He wasted no time.

"OK?" asked Mason disinterestedly.

"Fine," said Barney, dodged – and ran.

He was quite a fast runner and easily outpaced Kit Mason from the very beginning. A great wave of exhilaration passed through him. It was going to be easy after all. Dead easy. He would be home soon and be able to – then he heard Mason calling for Bruno.

At once Barney tried to double his speed, but he knew it was no good. He didn't stand a chance against the Alsatian. Nevertheless he ran as he had never run before, his heart pounding, determined not to look back. For a while he could hear nothing – no barking, no yelping. The desire to look back became over-whelming and he turned. It was fatal. Bruno was bounding along behind him, and Kit Mason was jogging a hundred metres behind. Running furiously, Barney turned the corner and was on the last stretch down to the beach where the sailing dinghy had been drawn up. He had about fifty metres to cover but already he could hear Bruno close behind him. Would the Alsatian shadow him all the way down to the beach, or would he spring, dragging him to the ground?

"Go, boy!"

Barney heard the command, turned, ran backwards and fell. He lay on his back on the hard tarmac, panting while Bruno stood over him. The dog was panting too.

"I saved your life. Now leave me alone," muttered Barney, suspecting that Bruno would be more likely to remember the stones he had thrown at him.

But instead of attacking him Bruno merely licked his face, standing feet apart without growling. Nevertheless, Barney decided not to move.

"You idiot!" said Kit Mason as he ran up. "Get off, boy!"

Bruno backed off and Barney got shakily to his feet. "You can't keep me against my will."

Mason did not reply as he grabbed Barney's arm and marched him back to the stranded *Rose*.

The morning dragged by as Barney, Alice and Jamie lay around in the hold while Kit Mason sat in the wheelhouse with Bruno. As he'd feared, rather than pleasing Alice by his attempt to escape, Barney had made her very angry.

"You ran out on us," she snapped, and Jamie, delighted she was siding with him for once, stirred the situation for all it was worth.

"Yeah, you were chicken, weren't you? Couldn't see it through," he crowed. "What about them yobbos still lurking about?"

"I was going for help." Barney grimly defended

himself, but inside he was in despair. "I was going to get the police – to stop him and Dr James, whether they're working together or not."

"Well, you blew it," Alice said unsympathetically. "And now we're worse off than before."

"Yeah," Jamie chipped in. "Now he won't give a damn about us."

But despite this gloomy prediction Mason had made them coffee and toast, although there wasn't much of it and they were starving. The monkeys grew friendlier, running about the floor, dancing and darting around them.

At about twelve they heard a klaxon blast out twice and a few minutes later Kit Mason appeared at the hatch.

"They're here. Early." His voice was expression-less.

No one said anything.

"I want you to do exactly what I say."

Still no one said anything.

"Yes?" Mason's voice had a threatening note to it now.

"OK," said Jamie eventually. "We're listening."

"My colleagues will come on board and remove the monkeys. Please help them."

"And then we're free to go?" asked Barney.

"Yes." Mason hesitated. "You're free to go." Alice looked at Barney in relief and his spirits soared, but Jamie seemed to be suffering from a sense of anti-climax. "I thought I was going with you. That we was going up the Thames together."

Kit looked a bit crestfallen. "Well, I've other things to attend to now."

"What other things?" Alice was deeply suspicious.

"I'm sorting a few things out and joining the boat at Ore Creek. They're going to put in for me."

"What do you want to go there for?" said Alice. "You've done your bit there now."

"Yes. But I must go back to the lab."

"Again? Why?" Jamie sounded amazed.

"And any of you are welcome to join me."

"But *why*?" insisted Alice.

"If you come with me, you'll see the state Dr James's animals are in."

"Are you going to grab some more then?" asked Jamie.

"No. I just want to take some photographs. I'm doing this job properly."

Alice looked at him for a long time, during which there was total silence. "Why were you joking with Dr James? Why were you so friendly with him?" she said at last.

"We were just doing things in a gentlemanly fashion," he replied.

Jamie gave a roar of raucous laughter. "It's up to the others if they go with you, but I'm going back to me dad. All right? I can outrun Tommy if he's still around."

"As long as you don't grass," said Mason.

"You couldn't do anything to me if I did."

"I can shut you up pretty effectively," said Mason. He opened his wallet and peeled off some ten-pounds notes. "Thirty now, and seventy when I'm safely up the Thames. Notes in a registered envelope?" He gave Jamie a contemptuous look.

"How do I know you'll send 'em?"

"How do I know you won't shop me?"

Jamie nodded.

"Get going then, and watch out for Baby-Face and his mate. They won't give up that easy."

"I can handle it." Jamie started up the ladder.

"Wait –" Alice was staring up at him.

"What's up?"

"Take care," she said.

Jamie smiled and for the first time Barney saw that he cared for her, in his own way. "We'll try and sort something out at home," he said. "Something better than we had before – when this is all over."

She nodded and he shifted his gaze to Barney. "You've been a good mate to her," he said.

"You coming, Alice, or not?" asked Mason quietly.

"Yes," she said equally quietly. "I'm coming."

"Barney?"

"OK," he replied reluctantly.

Mason began to climb the ladder.

"Why did you agree to go?" hissed Barney.

"I want to see what he's up to," replied Alice impatiently.

"It could be dangerous."

"Don't come then," she said. "It's up to you."

"If you're going," replied Barney, "so am I."

She grinned and his spirits soared.

Chapter Ten

The Animal Rights group arrived with the containers a few minutes later. They were two middle-aged men who looked rather like jobbing gardeners and worked at about the same pace. Slowly Barney and Alice helped them to collect up the frantic monkeys. The containers were large and roomy and there were not many animals in each. Eventually the job was finished and they came out on deck. It was just after one and both Alice and Barney blinked in the early afternoon sunshine after being imprisoned for so many hours below. Another trawler had been drawn up just behind the *Rose* and they loaded the monkeys into this.

"We'll be going then," said the slightly younger man and Mason nodded briskly. He looked at his watch.

"I need three hours. The tide will be full in Ore Creek by then. Come and pick me up."

"It's risky."

"I know, but it's a final embellishment I want."

What was it? Barney wondered. Would he force the Animal Rights men to unload the monkeys and return them to Dr James? Just what kind of devious game was Mason playing now? He looked at Alice and knew she was thinking the same. Should they warn the two men or what?

"You could blow the whole thing," said the older man.

"I shan't do that," said Kit Mason forcefully.

"You could have taken those photographs last time."

"Had a problem with the camera." Never had Kit Mason sounded so phoney. But the Animal Rights team either had no time to argue or were prepared to give him the benefit of the doubt.

"Let's get on with it then," said the younger man.

"We'll sail across," said Alice as the Animal Rights trawler disappeared from view. "We've got the dinghy."

Barney felt a stab of disappointment, remembering the idyllic sail of the previous day when everything had been so magical and they had been so close. Surely Mason had his own superior cruiser tucked away somewhere? But it seemed he hadn't.

"I didn't bring it," he explained. "Not wishing to draw attention to me and the *Rose* I bicycled over the bridge with Bruno running behind." He paused. "So it would quicker if I could come with you."

That's it, thought Barney, and it was. Half an hour later, Alice was at the helm and they were sailing before a light breeze towards Ore Creek on the mainland. Barney had hoped she would give him the helm, but she seemed determined to put herself in charge of the boat.

Kit Mason and Bruno crouched uneasily midships. Bruno stared out at the sea as if he wanted to drink it all. They were a silent company. The afternoon was fine and warm and the water scudded under the keel with a little trickling sound.

"You must try and believe me," said Mason. He looked white and pinched as if the strain of it all was really getting to him. "I'm not in league with Dr James and I'm not being paid by Animal Rights. And another thing I'm not – is a journalist."

They both looked at him in surprise.

"Then what are you?" asked Alice coldly.

"I'm an Animal Rights activist – that's all."

"So why are you working alone?" She was still cold.

"Because that was the plan. Only one of us should take the full risk."

"But you can't – I mean – what's your work?" asked Barney.

"I sell insurance."

They both stared at him unbelivingly. Then Alice said:

"I just don't know what to think."

"I can prove everthing to you. By tonight."

"How?" she asked.

"I'll have people vouch for me. Top people." He sounded rather childish and Barney stole a glance at Alice. She shook her head impatiently and he knew that she didn't believe Kit Mason either.

The tide was running out and the creek was almost dry. They sailed between high mud banks over which they could hardly see. A few sea birds patrolled the ridges: waders and cormorants who looked at them askance as the dinghy invaded their retreat. All three of them had fallen silent again, and Barney was experiencing a growing feeling of dread. He was sure that something really awful was going to happen. He wondered what Alice was thinking, sitting at the tiller, looking so calm and sure of herself. He suddenly realised that there was a similarity between her and Kit Mason. Both of them had a really confident exterior most of the time, but in rare moments when it evaporated they seemed lost and afraid.

"Are we near?" she asked, her voice sounding dangerously loud in the silence of the creek.

"It's at the end, by the old railway station."

Gradually a tall Victorian house came into view and the creek faded away into a matted thicket. Above the house rose a shabby signal and part of an old platform ran into a bed of reeds. A bird called plaintively and beyond the house they could see a jumbled collection of sheds and outbuildings.

"That's it," whispered Mason. "That's the lab."

"Are you sure there's no one there?"

"According to Dr James."

"Why should he tell you that?" asked Barney.

"Because I've arranged to meet him here," said Mason with a smile like a naughty schoolboy. Barney's heart sank. He had sprung yet another surprise on them, and was obviously enjoying seeing their expressions.

Alice was the first to recover. "What the hell are you up to now?" she rasped.

"That's what I was laughing about." He held their eyes, smiling still.

"I don't understand," said Barney miserably, really upset that his worst fears had come true.

"Dr James thinks he's going to buy me off."

"What will he think when he sees *us*?" asked Alice woodenly.

"He won't mind. After all, the lab's perfectly legal."

"So why have you *really* brought us here?" asked Alice.

"To prove to you that I am what I say I am."

"I don't believe you," said Alice. "You're out for yourself, that's all. You said we'd come here to take photographs. You won't be able to take any if you're meeting Dr James."

"I most certainly will, and Dr James will be in every one of them."

"You don't for one moment think he'll agree to that?" said Alice. She was almost scoffing at him now.

Kit Mason tapped his jerkin pocket. "I've got a minature camera in here; it fixes on to a wristwatch. I'll be able to snap away without him being any the wiser."

"Who do you think you are, James Bond?" Alice laughed, but her laughter was brittle with sarcasm. At once Kit Mason stopped smiling and Barney thought he caught a glimpse of defencelessness in his eyes, quickly replaced by a flash of anger.

"Let's see it then," said Barney, trying to imitate Alice's sarcasm but failing.

"I don't have to prove anything to you kids." For the first time Mason openly lost his temper. Maybe it was fatigue, maybe it was pride, thought Barney. Maybe it's because he expected us to believe in him. But how could we? Just how could we?

"Who the hell do you think you are?"

"You have to prove *everything*," returned Alice sharply. "You said you would."

But Kit Mason was now beside himself with sudden rage. "I don't have to show you anything. You can damn well take it or leave it. Accept me at face value or not at all."

"You have so many faces," said Alice. "It's impossible to know which is which."

"Ship ahoy!" Dr James, looking as calm as ever, stepped out from the tall, dark house. His voice was hearty and booming. "I see you've brought our young friends." He sounded as if he had invited them to a Sunday School play. "I've got good news for you, young lady."

"What?"

"Your father is pulling along nicely. Breathing much better and no sign of pneumonia."

He made Alice feel guilty that she had not stayed at her father's bedside – Barney could see that. But he could also see that she was very relieved.

"Where's your brother?" he added.

"Gone to my dad."

"Good. Now come alongside. You must have had a long sail. Can I get you a cup of tea?"

"No thanks," said Alice.

"Oh, do have one, then I can run you to the hospital." His bedside manner was at its most convincing. "In a way I'm glad you've come," he said as they floated towards him. "Mr Mason saw sense in the end. I'm also pleased to have the opportunity to show you round the lab. You'll find it very – humane."

"You're paying him off, aren't you?" said Barney.

"Well, I'm going to give him a small fee not to trouble us again. I suppose it's wrong but the world isn't a perfect place as you know, and Mr Mason here is not quite the idealist he cracks himself up to be."

Kit Mason was sitting in the stern, looking disgruntled. He reached for Bruno as if to find comfort. The dog nuzzled up to him. Dr James made fast the line and helped Alice out first.

"So you've come to the big, bad wolf, my dear?" He laughed as she shook herself free of him. "I don't think you'll find my lair as unpleasant as you imagine."

Dr James opened the door of a low concrete building and ushered them inside. There was the low hum of some kind of generator and a battery of scientific equipment that was quite unlike anything Barney had seen before. The long room was divided into sections, each with its own set of tubes, pipes, instruments, bottles and computers. As they walked down, Barney and Alice could see mice scuttling in one cage, rats in another and what looked like grass snakes in a tank. Everything was clean, functional and incomprehensible.

Out of the corner of his eye, Barney saw Kit Mason raise his arm and presumed that he had fitted the tiny camera he had talked about to his wristwatch. If he was to be believed, that is – and he probably wasn't. Everything appeared to be false now. Nothing and nobody was what they seemed – Mason, James, even the laboratory.

"So there's nothing very sinister in here, is there?" Dr James's voice was bright and confiding. "Everything done here is humane, and every experiment benefits a human being in some vital way." He sounded as if he had made this speech many times before and was bringing it out for another airing.

Outside Bruno began to bark.

"Hang on." Mason went towards the door and opened it. "Quiet, boy."

"What's up?" There was a tiny edge of unease to Dr James's voice.

"Nothing. Nobody around. He must have seen a rabbit or something."

"Now," said Dr James, "let's settle our dues." He went into a partitioned office and came out with a cheque book. He began to write. As he did so, he said, "And you'll be returning the monkeys to me –" he looked at his watch – "in about an hour's time."

"If you drive to Harty Ferry in your car I'll transfer the crates."

"And there will be no problem with your colleagues?"

"I'll settle them."

"Financially, I assume."

"You assume right." He was roving about the laboratory, occasionally looking at his watch, and Barney assumed he was either still photographing, or playing at it.

Outside Bruno began to bark again but this time no one took any notice.

"How can you do this?" Alice almost spat the words at Mason. "How can you take money after all the grand, good things you were going to do?"

"Needs must," said Mason.

Dr James flourished the cheque and turned to Alice. "I'm going to run you to the hospital to see your dad, and then I'll be back to meet the boat at Harty Ferry. With the cheque."

"Fine," said Mason. "You'll find the hand-over

will be very smooth, providing each of us keeps his side of the bargain."

"We will," replied Dr James briskly.

"You're such a swine!" said Alice. "Such a –"

"There's no point in indulging in abuse, young lady. Mr Mason and I have just struck a very sensible bargain, and that's all there is to it."

"I'm not going anywhere," said Alice. Suddenly she ran up to Dr James and ripped the cheque out of his hands, tearing it in tiny pieces and scattering them on the floor.

"That was stupid," said Mason. "Now he'll have to write out another one."

Looking thoroughly irritated, Dr James was just reaching for his cheque book again when there was a noise from a door at the back of the laboratory. It was no more than a shuffling sound but nevertheless the doctor put his finger to his lips. Signalling them to say nothing, he softly walked towards the door, grasped the handle and threw it open. Behind the door stood Tommy. In his hand he held a blowtorch, and he was smiling all over his baby-face. Behind him was the bearded Jason and two other well-built and menacing looking young men. They held a variety of weapons, ranging from a crowbar to a hammer and what looked like a very large starting handle.

"We've been listening to your deal," said Tommy truculently. "Now we want to make our own." With his battery of weapons, Tommy was clearly no longer afraid of Kit Mason. Instead, he was watching him intently, his little nugget eyes challenging.

Barney turned to see what Mason's reaction would be, but he was simply staring back at Tommy and his friends with a curious expression on his face, as if he was finally trapped.

"I didn't think we'd heard the last of you," Dr James said with a contemptuous smile. Turning to Kit Mason he added, "God knows how I could have been so stupid as to get involved with this lot."

"He's scum!" said Alice. "They all are. You must have been crazy. And on top of it all you didn't even pay them off."

Tommy stepped out of the corridor, closely followed by his three companions. "Let's have it then. Let's have what you owe us."

"You'll get nothing," said Dr James sharply. "Nothing at all. I told you to warn people off – not to try to kill them."

"We can go to the Bill – tell 'em you hired us. Tell 'em what you asked us to do." Tommy's little eyes flashed.

"I shall deny everything. It's your word against mine, and somehow I don't think you'll count for a lot. Not with the police."

"We got proof," said Tommy, unimpressed. "Lots of lovely proof."

"How's that?" Dr James looked slightly disconcerted. Barney watched Alice. She was standing with her fists clenched, her body taut. He hoped she was not going to do anything stupid.

"We got a photograph, haven't we?" Jason pulled out a blurred-looking print. He held it up. It showed

131

Dr James standing outside a pub near the sea wall in Whitstable, holding a pint of bitter. He was talking to the unmistakable figure of Tommy.

"And just in case that's not enough," said Tommy, "here's another one." The second was more incriminating. It showed Dr James again, but this time he was standing beside Kit Mason's barge. He was pointing at something and Tommy was laughing.

"Doesn't prove a thing," said Dr James, looking relieved. "Not a damn thing."

"We could send this to the Bill," Jason blustered. "Tell 'em what you were up to."

"And suppose, for one moment, they did take you seriously," scoffed Dr James. "If I was arrested, so would you be. All of you. And one of the charges could be attempted murder. Now stop playing damn stupid games, and get the hell out of this lab. I could ring the police now and have you arrested for breaking and entering."

They must have been waiting for us all this time, thought Barney. They could never have got past Bruno. Then he caught sight of Tommy's expression and a thrill of fear clutched at him. His baby-face was contorted with thwarted rage. He looked like a little child deprived of a toy and Barney realised that to Tommy, his ill-thought-out plan must have seemed like a real master stroke, something that would automatically extort money from Dr James. Now he was realising that it was all hopeless.

"Watch it!" yelled Alice. "Watch the torch!"

The flames leapt out before anyone realised what

was happening. Its heat was intense and Tommy directed it at a workbench covered in books and papers. Within seconds it was ablaze.

"OK?" yelled Tommy. "That good enough for you?" He pointed the torch at some telephone directories this time. In seconds the flames were leaping.

"For God's sake –" said Dr James, running for the fire extinguisher on the wall. "You must be crazy!"

That's the problem, thought Barney as he watched Tommy's laughing eyes. He *is* crazy.

He picked up the blowtorch again and began to run through the laboratory, followed by the other three. As Tommy started little pockets of fire, the others smashed equipment and glass cases. Soon white mice were running round the floor in desperate panic, and the flames were leaping towards them.

"Leave them alone!" shouted Alice, throwing herself at Jason. But he pushed her away easily and she fell backwards against an iron filing cabinet, cracking her head and lying still.

"Alice!" Barney ran towards her but Kit Mason was there first.

"You're not leaving here." Dr James was standing by the door, blocking the gang's exit. Meanwhile, thick black smoke was beginning to blanket the laboratory.

"Get out!" said Mason. "Just get out!"

Barney hesitated but Mason was already lifting

Alice up and running towards the door just as Jason hit Dr James in the stomach. He staggered and the gang, headed by a wildly cheering and laughing Tommy, made their departure. Still staggering, Dr James cannoned into Mason, but he pushed his way past, carrying Alice. Barney brought up the rear.

"You OK?" he asked. Dr James nodded and stumbled out after them into the wonderfully cleansing air outside. Alice opened her eyes as Mason laid her gently on the grass while a tongue of red flame burst out of the laboratory's roof, followed by rolling black smoke.

"There's a telephone box down the road!" yelled Mason to Dr James. "Get the fire brigade!" He looked down at Alice. "And an ambulance. Fast. And get back quickly," he added authoritatively.

"Where are you going?" rapped Dr James as Kit Mason turned towards the blazing building.

"Inside!" he yelled over his shoulder.

"Why?" asked Barney. "What the hell for?"

"There's a glass container with some rats in it. I'm going to get them out. I think that's the only cage Tommy left intact."

Barney stared at him in amazement as he dashed back.

Alice stood up shakily, holding her head. "Where's he gone?"

"Back inside."

"No! What for?"

"To rescue some rats."

"Rats! So he was right after all," she said in

distress. "He *was* fooling Dr James. He *was* taking photographs. We shouldn't have doubted him."

"How do you make that out?" asked Barney.

"Who but a real animal lover would go back in there, just for some rats?" She began to cry and Bruno set up a mournful howling.

They waited and waited while the roaring of the flames and dark smoke intensified. But still Kit Mason did not emerge.

"I'm going in," said Alice, dragging herself towards the door.

"You're *not*!" yelled Barney, grabbing at her and trying to hold her back. Meanwhile, Bruno continued to howl despairingly.

Suddenly someone shouted: "Stop! What the hell's going on?"

"He's in there!" Alice screamed. "Kit Mason went in, and he's not come out."

Barney suddenly recognised the two men as the Animal Rights protestors who had loaded the monkeys on to the trawler. Neither looked a likely rescuer, but they immediately dashed into the dense black smoke, calling out Kit Mason's name as they ran.

After what seemed an endless wait they dragged him out, almost unconscious. But under his arm, safely rescued, was a container holding two large and terrified rats.

"They're on their way," said Dr James breathlessly,

reappearing from the road. Taking in the situation, he ran towards Kit Mason and knelt down beside him. "He's breathing," he said, listening to his chest. "But he's got some bad burns. The ambulance should be here any minute now."

Sure enough, its siren could be heard, wailing over the marshes. Mason opened his eyes; they were suddenly alive in his smoke-blackened face. He began to cough.

"Take it easy," said Dr James. "Very easy. The ambulance is on its way. And what about you, young lady? Perhaps you should go to hospital to be on the safe side."

Ignoring him, Alice leant over Mason. "I'm sorry," she whispered.

"Sorry?" he rasped.

"We didn't believe you. We thought you'd done a deal."

Mason held up his wrist. "Very James Bond, but it's real." He looked up at Dr James. "I was photographing –" He dissolved into more coughing.

"Don't try to talk." Dr James didn't seem to register what Mason was saying, but shot a glance up at the blazing laboratory and shrugged. Bruno licked Mason's face and the rats huddled together – rather like the monkeys, Barney thought.

The ambulance arrived a few minutes ahead of the fire engines. Alice refused to go, but Kit Mason was lifted onto a stretcher. As he was taken aboard he gave a thumbs-up sign.

"Look after Bruno," he said to Alice and Barney. "Just for a few days." He waved and then disappeared into the ambulance, still managing to look faintly glamorous.

"What a risk!" said one of the Animal Rights men.

"We didn't know what to think," said Alice. "Didn't know whether he was a fake or not."

"He's no fake," replied the man.

"And he wasn't paid anything?" asked Barney miserably. "You weren't giving him £30,000?"

"£30,000? We haven't got that sort of money. Anyway, he wouldn't want to be *paid*. Not Kit Mason. He's not interested in money. All he owns is that barge and the sailing cruiser, and that's family money anyway."

"And he's not a journalist?" asked Alice.

"Or an insurance salesman?" said Barney.

The man laughed. "Kit could fool you into thinking he was all manner of things. He's a loss assessor actually, but there's one thing he's really interested in – Animal Rights. Look at the rats! He'd rescue a spider from the top of the Eiffel Tower if he thought it was being mistreated."

Barney and Alice were silent. It was left to Dr James to find words.

"He's a brave man," he said quietly. "Whether I agree with him or not, he's a brave man."

Epilogue

"Look at this," said Alice. She and Barney were strolling along the beach together with Bruno running at their heels. The patients were doing well: her father was due out of hospital at the end of the week and Kit Mason the middle of the next. Both were going to make complete recoveries, although Mason had been quite badly burned.

They stopped at a low wall overlooking the marshes. Sheep grazed contentedly on a still, warm weekend morning.

The main headline of the local paper read:

LOCAL YOUTHS ARRESTED:
ARSON AT LABORATORY

And much lower down there was a small paragraph under the heading:

LOCAL DOCTOR TAKES
EARLY RETIREMENT

"We never found out what the experiments were for," said Barney. "He wasn't much of a villain in the end. He just seemed to give up."

"He was weak, that's all," said Alice. "But at least we know that Kit was on the level," she added. "I suppose I shouldn't have doubted him. But he did behave in such an odd way at times, as if it was all a game. He liked games, and playing them almost wrecked him."

"I suppose everything'll be back the way it was now," said Barney regretfully.

"Not quite," replied Alice. She grabbed hold of him, planting a light kiss on his forehead. "You've been great! We can be friends now, can't we?"

Barney went red in the face. But inside his heart leapt as high as the gulls wheeling above them.

"You're welcome to come to my house," he said.

"And mine. I know it's not much of a place," Alice sighed, "but at least it'll be different now."

"I'll have to go back to London soon." Barney was despondent.

"Whitstable isn't that far," she said, "and you could always invite me up."

"I could," said Barney with sudden joy. "Yes, I really could!"